Who's the new girl?

"Hey, Brian," said a cute, dark-haired boy as he walked up to my locker partner. "Hey," the guy said to me.

"Hi," I said softly. Suddenly I was back to feeling kind of shy again.

"Hey, Salvador. Ready to roll?" Brian said to the guy.

"Ready like Freddy," Salvador replied, and gave me a grin.

"This is Elizabeth," Brian said. "My locker partner."

"Lucky," Salvador said, and I blushed.

"Nice to meet you," I managed to say.

Brian gave me a little eyebrow wiggle and shut the locker door. "See you," he said.

I took a deep breath. "See you." I looked at Salvador, so he'd know I meant him too.

"Yes, I hope to see you *soon*," Salvador replied, emphasizing the last word, and making me blush again. Brian gave Salvador a little shove, and the two of them walked down the hall. I stayed where I was for a second, pressed up against the security of my locker.

That went okay, I told myself. *See? The people here are nice. You'll make friends.*

I tried really hard to believe it.

SWEET VALLEY jr. high

Get Real

Written by
Jamie Suzanne

Created by
FRANCINE PASCAL

BANTAM BOOKS
NEW YORK · TORONTO · LONDON · SYDNEY · AUCKLAND

To Laurie Wenk

RL 4, 008-012

GET REAL

A Bantam Book / February 1999

Sweet Valley Junior High is a trademark of
17th Street Productions, a division of Daniel Weiss Associates, Inc.

Conceived by Francine Pascal.

Produced by 17th Street Productions,
a division of Daniel Weiss Associates, Inc.
33 West 17th Street, New York, NY 10011.

ISBN: 0-553-48603-9

Published simultaneously in the United States and Canada

PRINTED IN THE UNITED STATES OF AMERICA

OPM   0 9 8 7 6 5 4 3 2 1

Jessica

The day before I started junior high (in other words, the last day I could sleep in), my best friend, Lila Fowler, barged into my room and woke me up at nine o'clock by slapping a thick copy of *Seventeen* on my chest. She has a knack for being inhuman sometimes.

"Get up," Lila said. "We're going shopping."

I groaned and rolled over. The magazine slid to the floor.

Lila retrieved it. "Look," she said, waving it in front of my half-opened eyelids.

"Look at what?" I croaked.

"At what the model is wearing," Lila said impatiently, tapping the glossy cover. She'd obviously been awake for a while. Every light brown hair was in place, and her clothes were perfect, as always. "I want to get that exact outfit."

I gave up any hope of going back to sleep, given that Lila was now perched at the edge of my bed, and sat up. Lila thrust the *Seventeen* into my hands. It was one of those back-to-school issues, featuring a cover girl wearing a white blouse, green sweater vest, tan blazer, and kilt.

"She's wearing a kilt," I said.

"It's not a kilt," Lila corrected. "It's a tartan skirt. Plaid is very in this season."

It is? I thought. I looked at the magazine again. The girl did look terrific in that outfit. But models look good in anything—that's their job.

"Hurry," Lila said impatiently. "I want to get to the mall as soon as possible so we can both buy this outfit. Then you can wear it on your first day at Sweet Valley Junior High and I'll wear it my first day at Sweet Valley Middle School, and we'll be the best-dressed people in either place."

That's right, I thought. *I need to make a great impression on the first day of school.* See, we had just found out for sure that the Sweet Valley school districts had been rezoned. They had sent everyone a letter at the end of the summer, letting people know which they had been assigned to. My friends and I had spent the last two years at Sweet Valley Middle School. But when I opened my letter, I found out that I was going to a whole new school—Sweet Valley Junior High.

Naturally I immediately called everyone I knew to find out who was going where. And guess what? I'm the *only* one of my good friends who got rezoned. Same for my twin sister, Elizabeth. Plus, while Sweet Valley Middle School is for sixth to eighth grades, Sweet Valley Junior High is for seventh to ninth—so now Elizabeth and I weren't going to rule the school as eighth-graders, like I had planned.

I was way, way bummed . . . for about five seconds. Then I realized—this was the chance of a lifetime! *Hello?* There would be tons of new people to meet and tons of new guys to hang out with—*older* guys. It was going to be great.

I took another look at the *Seventeen* outfit. Even though I wasn't really wild about it, I trusted Lila's taste. Like I said before, she always looks great. And now that she and I were going to different schools, I could dress just like her and no one would know.

"Come on," Lila coaxed. "Don't you want to make a good impression?"

"Yes, but . . ." I hesitated. "It'll be expensive."

"You told me that your mom gave you and Elizabeth some money for school clothes," Lila said promptly. "I know you still have it."

Why do I always tell her everything? I was saving that money for a bunch of new clothes, not a single kilt. I knew Lila would just pay for her outfit with one of her dad's credit cards—

Jessica

he's one of the richest men in Sweet Valley, if not the known universe.

"I want us to wear the same thing," Lila said. "It'll be fun; nobody will know about it but us."

"Well . . . okay," I said, and got out of bed. As I brushed my hair and slipped into a T-shirt and pair of shorts, I briefly considered asking Elizabeth if she wanted to come with us. Then I decided against it. She and Lila don't really get along, and Elizabeth hadn't been herself since we found out about this new-school thing. It was weird—usually she always looks on the bright side of everything. I knew she had been looking forward to editing the SVMS paper and all that, but she really needed to get a grip. If I had a nickel for every time Elizabeth and I had talked about her junior-high fears in the past week, I'd—I'd be able to afford that *Seventeen* outfit.

I took the money my mom had given me out of my underwear drawer and put it in my pocket. "I'm ready."

We went downstairs, where I grabbed a banana and left a note for my mom so that she wouldn't go berserk and call the police if we were out all day.

Outside, we got on our bicycles. Lila put the copy of *Seventeen* on her bike rack.

"Maybe we can find a tartan that has a little purple in it," she said as we coasted down my driveway.

"Great idea," I said. Lila and I both belong to the Unicorn Club, which is made up of the prettiest and most popular girls at SVMS. We try to wear something purple every day.

I wished suddenly that just one other Unicorn was coming to junior high with me. Elizabeth wasn't a Unicorn, although she'd been asked. She thinks the Unicorns are a bunch of snobs—which is true, kind of—but they're also a lot of fun. "I can't believe I'll be the only Unicorn at Sweet Valley Junior High," I said.

"Lucky," Lila said with a sniff.

I gave her a sidelong glance. She was right, of course—I *was* lucky. I was going to make all new friends, while she was going to be doing the same thing as always. I felt a little sorry for her.

I pictured myself on the first day of school. Everyone would remark on my cutting-edge style. Cute guys would rush forward and introduce themselves. I would manage to make witty remarks and impress all of my teachers.

Suddenly I couldn't wait for the next twenty-four hours to pass. *Look out, Sweet Valley Junior High!* I thought. *Here comes Jessica Wakefield!*

Elizabeth

Even though dinner was miserable, I didn't want it to end. Because every minute that passed brought me closer to junior high—and closer to my identity as The New Girl with No Friends.

Jessica had called to say that she was still off with Lila in search of the *Seventeen* outfit and was going to grab a burger at the mall, so it was just me, my parents, and my older brother, Steven, sitting around the table.

Steven is sixteen, with brown hair and brown eyes, and apparently lots of girls think he's cute, judging by the number who call our house every minute of the day and night.

His main interest is cars and how he wants to buy one. The fact that Steven doesn't even have enough money to buy a *bicycle* doesn't stop him from reading the classified ads and talking about used cars all the time. It can be pretty boring. I don't know how the girls who call him keep from yawning.

"I saw a Honda this morning," he said to my dad. "Not too many miles."

I sighed. We were having meat loaf, which reminded me of something that a school cafeteria would serve, which reminded me that tomorrow I would be eating in a school cafeteria, but not the SVMS cafeteria, the junior-high one, where I wouldn't know anyone except Jessica. I sighed again.

"What's wrong, Elizabeth?" my mother asked.

"Oh, I'm just thinking about school tomorrow," I said. "All those strange people."

"You're pretty strange yourself," Steven said between mouthfuls of mashed potatoes, "so you should fit right in." Steven isn't big in the sympathy department, obviously.

"Honey, I keep telling you that there'll be other people from SVMS there," my mother said. "We can't be the only family that got rezoned."

No, it just seems like it, I thought. Sure, I knew people who had been rezoned. I just didn't know any of them *well.* But I said, "I guess you're right."

"Elizabeth, this new school is a great opportunity," my dad put in.

Suddenly I was really sorry I had brought up the subject because my dad has told me that the new school is "a great opportunity" about ninety-nine times in the past week. I'm not exaggerating.

Elizabeth

"I know, Dad," I said. I cast a pleading look at Steven, who—for once—took pity on me.

"Dad," Steven said, interrupting before my dad could go through his whole "great opportunity" speech. "If I could borrow the car tomorrow, I could drive the twins to school and they wouldn't have to take the bus."

The bus! I'd completely forgotten that Jessica and I were going to have to be on the bus by six forty-five. When we were going to SVMS, we didn't even get up until six forty-five!

At least they were "easing us back into school" by starting on a Wednesday. *Just three days till the weekend,* I thought.

"I need my car tomorrow." My dad turned to my mom. "What about you, Alice?"

"I'll need mine too," she said. "Besides, I think the girls should get used to the bus."

I didn't like the sound of that particular sentence, but before I could respond, Jessica burst through the kitchen door, carrying about five shopping bags.

"We found it!" Jessica sang out. "I'm going to go upstairs and try it on. Come on, Lizzie."

Mom shook her head. "Jessica, Elizabeth is eating her dinner."

"That's okay, Mom. I want to see what Jessica bought." I pushed back my chair. "I'm finished anyway."

I carried my half-full plate into the kitchen, then followed Jessica upstairs. She looked a little hot and sweaty, but happy.

"I'll change in the bathroom," she said, hurrying inside with all her bags. "So you get the full effect." I heard the rustle of tissue paper. "We had to go to about five million stores," Jessica continued from behind the closed bathroom door. "But it was worth it."

"Do you know what time we have to catch the bus tomorrow?" I asked, sitting down on her bed.

"What?" she called.

"I said, do—," I started, but just then Jessica threw open the door.

"Ta da!"

I was suddenly speechless.

Jessica was wearing a white blouse, white kneesocks, and a tan blazer—that much looked normal. But she was also wearing this incredibly bright purple-and-green-plaid skirt that flared a little bit. She looked like—Jessica looked like—

It's kind of a long story, but there's this very corny restaurant in town called Ye Olde Scottish Taverne, and in the summertime they hire a big fat man to wear a kilt and play the bagpipes. Well, Jessica looked like a younger, skinnier, more colorful version of him.

"What do you think?" she asked eagerly. "It

Elizabeth

was Lila's idea to get purple tartan instead of green and yellow." Jessica twirled around, and I actually got a little nauseated from watching the green and purple in motion.

"Are you sure you want to wear that on the first day of school?" I asked carefully. The skirt ruined even the nice, normal parts of the outfit.

"Lizzie! That's the whole point, to make a good impression," Jessica said impatiently. "Lila's going to wear hers too."

That made me feel a little better. Lila wouldn't wear something that wasn't cool. Maybe I just didn't have the fashion sense to appreciate it.

I realized that I had no idea what I was going to wear and sighed.

"Quit sighing," Jessica instructed. "This new school is a great opportunity."

I fell backward onto her bed, covering my face with my hands. "Please don't turn into Dad," I said.

"Oh, all right," Jessica said. "But you'll see."

I sat up again.

Jessica was admiring herself in the mirror. "This outfit cost me all the money Mom gave me," she said. "But it was worth it."

I nodded, privately thinking that if she ran low on cash, she could always get a part-time job at Ye Olde Scottish Taverne.

A n n a

"Hello?"

"Hi, Anna. What's up?"

I laughed. "Well, not that much since you left my house half an hour ago." Actually, I had been cleaning out my closet in an effort to find something decent to wear to school the following day. I gave up when I realized that the only outfit I own that doesn't have a hole in it is my old Brownie uniform. I try to be careful with my clothes, but somehow they always get messed up the first time I wear them. "What have you been doing?"

"Thinking about how much I don't want to go to school tomorrow," he said.

"School isn't so bad," I told him. Actually, I happen to like school, but I knew Salvador needed some reassurance. "We'll still get to hang out and do lots of fun stuff, like watching videos on Saturday night."

"Yeah, but we could do that *every* night during the summer." I thought it was pretty funny that

Anna

he said that, because we *hadn't* watched videos
every night during the summer. In fact, for the
past month Salvador had been spending a lot of
time with his cousin Mark. I had been extremely
happy when Mark had finally gone home to
Austin last week so I could have my best friend
back. I mean, I could've hung out with the two
of them, but when Salvador was with his guy
friends, he acted . . . different.

"We'll make Saturday nights special. I'll make
toffee popcorn."

"Okay. I love that."

Then I had an inspiration. "Why don't you
join the *Spectator* with me?" I asked. I was really
hoping to make the *Spec* this year—that's our
school paper. I hadn't made it last year, but I'd
been writing a lot over the summer, and I knew
I was getting better.

"No way. I don't want to write stupid articles
about speaking dogs."

I stared at the phone, confused. "What are
you talking about?" I asked.

"Last year Charlie wrote an article that was
supposed to be from a dog's point of view,"
Salvador replied. "It was supposed to make everyone think about animal rights."

"Well, see," I told him. "You should try out so
you can write more intelligent articles."

12

"A monkey could write more intelligent articles. They should have gotten a real dog to write that article—it would have been far more intelligent."

I had to grin in spite of myself. "So you'll join me?" I asked him.

"Maybe."

"Good." I glanced back into my closet and thought about my most pressing problem. "Listen, what are you wearing tomorrow?"

"Uh-oh." Salvador sounded wary. "I think it's time to hang up now."

"Why?" I demanded.

"Because this is a girly conversation." I rolled my eyes. Salvador hates "girly stuff." You would think he'd be over it, considering his best friend *is* a girl, but lately he's been really into doing more and more "guy stuff." Yet another example of a way in which growing up sucks.

"Salvador," I said, as patiently as possible, "I have to have this conversation with someone, and you're my only alternative."

"Well, I refuse. I can put my grandmother on the phone and you can discuss it with her."

"Okay."

"Seriously?" He sounded surprised.

"Sure." Salvador's grandmother has good taste, and I was desperate to come up with a decent outfit.

"All right. Grandma? Anna wants to talk to you!"

13

Wednesday Morning
First Day of School

6:15 A.M.   Elizabeth looks so miserable that Mr. Wakefield calls her "Little Mary Sunshine" in an effort to cheer her up. It does not work.

6:17 A.M.   Salvador del Valle's alarm goes off—loudly. Salvador punishes it with a hearty slap.

6:19 A.M.   Jessica French-braids her hair.

6:20 A.M.   Anna Wang puts on the outfit she and Salvador's grandmother decided on the day before—a green dress and black sandals. Upon zipping up the dress, Anna discovers a rather large hole at the seam.

6:25 A.M.   Jessica places her hair in bun.

6:28 A.M.   Salvador's grandmother comes into his room and attempts to wake him up by adjusting the blinds so that the sun shines directly into his eyes. Salvador retaliates by placing his pillow over his face.

6:30 A.M.   Jessica brushes her hair and leaves it down.

6:31 A.M.   Anna puts on a black skirt and white shirt, then begins hunting for her sandals. She never finds the left one.

6:35 A.M.   Jessica is in the kitchen, cleaning out her backpack from last year so that she can put her new school supplies in it.

"What is that?" Elizabeth asks, pointing to a greenish square Jessica has placed on the counter.

It used to be a ham sandwich," Jessica says. "But now it has its own ecosystem, complete with food chain."

6:45 A.M. Elizabeth and Jessica stumble to the bus stop, just awake enough to be miserably tired.

7:04 A.M. Salvador's grandmother comes back into his room and asks him if he's sure he's awake because she's going out. Salvador says of course he's sure—do sleeping persons sit up and hold conversations?

7:06 A.M. Anna gives up and puts on black jeans and a red blouse.

7:15 A.M. Salvador wakes up, looks at the clock, says something in Spanish not printable here—and leaves for school still wearing the T-shirt he slept in.

Elizabeth

I let Jessica climb aboard the bus first since she always likes to choose the seat. As we passed aisle after aisle of happy, chatty friends, my say-what-you-really-feel twin turned around and told me, "Nobody cool is here anyway."

"Jessica!" I whispered. I hated to think that people would be thinking that *we* weren't cool, especially since Jessica looked like a lavender leprechaun who'd just escaped from prep school.

She shrugged. "We can talk to each other."

I nodded. Jessica and I finally found a seat at the back, and almost immediately she fell asleep with her head on my shoulder. I sighed. So much for talking to each other.

I glanced around the bus, but everyone was chatting excitedly and/or throwing things. No one paid any attention to us. I pulled a novel out of my backpack and read that until we got to school.

Elizabeth

Jessica rubbed her eyes and looked around as we walked up to the junior high. It was a sprawling, two-story, brown-brick building with small windows, which made it look kind of like a prison. Or maybe that was just my take on it. Our old school had a fountain in front of it, but here there was only a big stretch of grass that everyone trampled instead of using the sidewalk. Inside, though, it looked like any other school, with tiled floors and long rows of tall lockers.

Jessica pointed at a sign. "We have to follow the arrows."

The cafeteria was about ten times the size of the one at SVMS. The tables were all labeled with the letters of the alphabet. Jessica and I headed for the one marked W.

A woman wearing a blue tracksuit with white piping was sitting behind the table. She had a whistle around her neck and a sticky label on the breast of her tracksuit that said, Hi! My Name Is Miss Scarlett. Miss Scarlett was the kind of woman who people would say was "handsome" rather than "beautiful" because of the severe expression on her face. I would have called her "scary."

She barely glanced at us. "Name?"

"Jessica Wakefield," Jessica said.

The woman began flipping through a stack of papers.

17

Elizabeth

"Elizabeth Wakefield," I told her, knowing that our forms would be together.

"Sisters?" she said absently.

"No relation," Jessica said.

Miss Scarlett looked at her sharply, but Jessica kept a perfectly straight face. Miss Scarlett frowned.

"Here are your schedules, girls," she said, handing us slips of paper. "The first bell rings at seven twenty-five, and class starts five minutes later."

Jessica had taken both her schedule and mine and was scanning them. "Where's our homeroom?" she asked.

"Sweet Valley Junior High doesn't have homeroom," Miss Scarlett said.

I couldn't believe it. "No homeroom!" I blurted.

Miss Scarlett gave me a chilly smile. "This is *junior high,*" she said in the same sort of voice she would have used if I'd said, *No nap time!*

I blushed. I hoped none of the other students lining up at the other tables had heard that. I glanced around, but everyone else was just collecting their schedules and talking to their friends. I saw one or two familiar SVMS faces looking as awkward as I felt—but nobody whose name I knew.

Miss Scarlett rummaged in a metal box and produced two more slips of paper. "These are your locker assignments and combinations," she said. "Do you know how to work a combination lock?"

Boy, I guess she thought we really were babies. I could see Jessica opening her mouth to say something, so I said, "Yes, we know," and steered her into the hall.

"Jeez," Jessica said, shaking off my hand. "What a weirdo."

"I know," I said patiently. "Could I have my schedule back, please?"

"Hold on," she said, comparing it to hers. "These schedules are hard to read, but it looks like we don't have any classes together."

"You're kidding!" I said, alarmed. I grabbed the papers out of her hands and studied them. "And our lockers are nowhere near each other."

I felt like crying. Instead I took a few deep breaths and tried to pull myself together.

The first bell rang.

"Oh no," Jessica groaned. "If I can't find my locker, I'm going to be late! See you at lunch if not before!" she called, already walking down the hall, peering at locker numbers.

I stared after her a minute and then looked again at the paper in my hand. Noticing that my locker number started with a two, I began climbing the stairs in search of my locker. And when I found it, there was some guy with long blond hair putting all his books in it!

Just what I need, I thought. *To get into a fight*

19

over lockers before first period has even started.

I took a deep breath and marched up to the guy. "I'm afraid you've made a mistake," I said, trying to sound official. "This is my locker."

The guy just laughed. "You must be Elizabeth."

I was startled. "How did you know?"

"It's written inside our locker," he said, pointing to a strip of masking tape that said Elizabeth Wakefield. Above it was another strip that said Brian Rainey.

"That's me." Brian smiled. "We're locker partners."

"Oh," I said, embarrassed.

"We just started having partners last year when the school got so crowded. It was cheaper than replacing all the lockers with the short kind. Top shelf or bottom shelf?" he asked.

"Bottom, I guess," I said, since Brian was taller.

"I have two favors to ask you," Brian said, flipping his long blond hair out of his eyes.

"Hey, Bri," a girl called as she passed.

"Hey, what's up?" Brian answered. He was still smiling when he looked back at me, and I relaxed about a millimeter. I'd been kind of worried that everyone at junior high would have their set friends already and wouldn't want to make new ones. That's how people were at SVMS. But Brian seemed ready to be friends with anyone.

"The two favors?" I prompted.

"Oh yeah," he said. "The first thing is, can I ask you not to put up a makeup mirror? Because all my friends will laugh at me if you do."

I laughed. "No problem."

"The second favor," Brian said, "is that I'd like to stick all our used chewing gum to the inside of the locker door so that we can use cultures from it for extra credit in biology next semester."

That sounded pretty disgusting, but he was so nice that I said, "Sure."

Brian took the piece of gum he was chewing and stuck it to the inside of the door. "Cool," he said. "If we end up in the same bio class, we can be biology partners if you want."

"That would be great," I replied.

Brian unloaded his books into the locker. "Well, see you around, Elizabeth."

"Oh, wait," I said. "Can you explain my schedule to me? I don't get it."

"Sure." He looked over my shoulder. "We have 'block schedules,' which means that we only have three classes per day plus gym, but it's a different three classes every other day."

"Three classes?" I asked. "That's all?"

Brian laughed. "Yeah, but each one lasts an hour and a half."

I groaned.

"It's rough," Brian said. "But you get used to it."

"Hey, Brian," said a cute dark-haired boy as he walked up to us. "Hey," the guy said to me.

"Hi," I said softly. Suddenly I was back to feeling kind of shy again.

"Hey, Salvador. Ready to roll?" Brian said to the guy.

"Ready like Freddy," Salvador replied, and gave me a grin.

"This is Elizabeth," Brian said. "My locker partner."

"Lucky," Salvador said, and I blushed.

"Nice to meet you," I managed to say.

Brian gave me a little eyebrow wiggle and shut the locker door. "See you," he said.

I took a deep breath. "See you." I looked at Salvador so he'd know I meant him too.

"Yes, I hope to see you *soon,*" Salvador replied, emphasizing the last word and making me blush again. Brian gave Salvador a little shove, and the two of them walked down the hall. I stayed where I was for a second, pressed up against the security of my locker.

That went okay, I told myself. *See? The people here are nice. You'll make friends.*

I tried really hard to believe it.

Jessica

Well, my locker partner turned out to be this hyper little skinny guy with big brown eyes. He looked as much like a puppy as it is possible to look like a puppy and still be human. Actually, puppies are cuter, but that's beside the point.

"Hello, I'm Ronald Rheece," he said, and held his hand out in front of him.

It took a full minute before I realized that he wanted to shake hands since the only other person I ever shake hands with is the minister in church. But it would have been rude to keep standing there, staring at his hand as though it were an alien tentacle, so I eventually said, "Jessica Wakefield," and shook hands (glancing sideways to make sure that nobody was seeing this). I had hoped I'd be able to find some really cute guy to explain my schedule to me, but I guessed I'd have to settle for what I was given.

Jessica

"Listen, can you tell me—," I started, but Ronald cut me off.

"My favorite subject is math, and my hobbies are building castles out of matchsticks, constructing a ham radio using only toaster parts, and trying to find the world's largest prime number. I'm eleven months younger than the youngest eighth-grader because I skipped the second grade." Was he reading from a cue card? I almost turned around to see if someone was holding one up.

"Uh—" I said, but he wasn't paying attention, so I just waited for him to run out of steam and hoped nobody would think that the reason I was standing here and talking to this guy was because we were actually friends.

"I belong to the chess club and the debate team," Ronald continued. "And we won't have many classes together because I take a special bus over to the high school for advanced calculus in the mornings."

"Well, good for you," I said (heartily relieved about the fact that we wouldn't have a lot of classes together). I meant to sound sarcastic, but I guess he didn't get it because he just looked really proud. "Can I unpack my books now?" I asked.

"Oh, sure," Ronald said. "I took the lower shelf."

Considering that I topped Ronald by about

24

five inches, it seemed unfair to protest. "Fine," I told him.

"I can tell you an easy way to memorize our locker combination," Ronald said. "It's all prime numbers."

"Well, thanks," I said, trying not to roll my eyes.

"See?" Ronald said. "Seven-three-thirteen."

"Yes," I replied. "I know what a prime number is."

"But do you know what a *quark* is?" Ronald asked in a challenging voice.

Boy, Ronald Rheece must be the weirdest person in the whole school. At least, I *hoped* he was the weirdest person in the school. The thought that there might be someone weirder than Ronald at SVJH was actually kind of frightening. It was clear I was going to have to conduct my social life somewhere other than my locker.

"Doesn't your bus leave soon?" I asked.

Ronald completely forgot about quarks and gave a little yip. "Oh gosh!" he said. "See you later, Jessica!"

"See ya," I said. I shut my (our?) locker and went off to find my first class, which was algebra.

This is going to sound dumb, but until I actually walked into room 103, I don't think I realized that I wouldn't have any *friends* at this school. I don't know what I expected, but it sure wasn't this class full of strangers, already divided up into pairs and groups, sitting together and talking and laughing, no one even giving me so much as a glance. I'd forgotten how hard it is to walk up to someone and start a conversation as opposed to having *them* come up to *you*, which is how things usually went for me at SVMS.

I took a deep breath. I couldn't be the only person who got rezoned, could I? I bit my lip, desperately wishing that Lila were here with me. Then suddenly I saw Sally Bank and hurried down the aisle toward her.

There was an empty seat next to her, and I slid into it gratefully. "Hi, Sal—"

"I'm saving that for Deena," Sally said, as if I should have known better than to sit in Deena's seat.

"Oh, I'm . . . sorry," I said, but Sally didn't smile or anything. I wondered if she was still mad about the time I said that her new haircut made her look like a pineapple. She *would* hold a grudge about something like that.

"I guess I'll sit in back, then," I said, trying to make it sound like it was my idea.

Sally didn't say anything, and my face began to feel hot. I hoped nobody had overheard that little exchange. I couldn't believe I'd just been dissed by Pineapple Head!

I chose a seat at the very end of a row, with empty desks on all sides of it. That way I figured some other people could come sit next to me, but no one did, and a minute later the bell rang and the teacher came in.

"Hello, folks, I'm Mr. Wilfred," the teacher said. He was tall and bald, and he had one of those monotone voices that would be practically impossible to listen to even if he were talking about something really interesting (which he wasn't). "Does anyone have any questions about our new block schedules?" he said. "Because the bell will still ring every fifty minutes, but class won't be over. . . ."

I tuned him out and started studying the other people in the class. The only person I recognized besides Sally was Deena Spence, the girl she'd been saving the seat for. Deena was this goody-goody type who used to work on the Sweet Valley *Sixers* with Elizabeth back in sixth grade. If she and Sally wanted to hang out together, fine. They weren't the kind of people I wanted to be friends with anyway. I wanted to make cool friends.

Friends exactly like the girl who was sitting a few seats in front of me.

The girl was really pretty, with shoulder-length brown hair. She was sitting sideways in her chair, and I could see that she had a tiny ski-jump nose and very long eyelashes. Her eyebrows were darker than her hair and very arched.

Mr. Wilfred began calling role, and I couldn't wait to find out the girl's name. "Lucy Frells?" he called, and the girl raised one tan arm lazily.

"It's Lacey," she said.

"Casey?" Mr. Wilfred asked.

"*Lacey,*" the girl said distinctly, as if she were talking to an idiot. (Of course, Mr. Wilfred was *acting* like an idiot, but I still wouldn't have the courage to talk to him that way.)

Lacey (cool name!) waited until Mr. Wilfred had his back to us, and then she turned around and put a note on another girl's desk. I leaned forward and smiled at her. I meant it to be a friendly look, but she didn't smile back. She just studied me for a moment, looking at my hair and my face and my clothes—*my clothes!*

The smirk on her face made me suddenly aware of how bright the plaid skirt was. I smoothed the skirt over my legs nervously. Was it too bright? But Lila had chosen it.

Lacey was wearing jeans and a sleeveless white blouse. I vowed to wear something similar tomorrow. I was roasting in all this scratchy wool anyway.

"I'm not going to make a seating chart," Mr. Wilfred said, writing on a piece of paper. "You

28

can just sit where you are for the rest of the marking period."

I wanted to throw something at him. No seating chart! Now I would have to sit surrounded by empty desks for six weeks. Well, I'd try to change seats next time—maybe Mr. Wilfred wouldn't notice. *And thankfully this class is almost over,* I thought, *so I can go to the next one and try to sit next to Lacey.* I wondered how I could explain my outfit. Maybe I could say that I was a model and this was what I wore for some back-to-school fashion shoot.

The bell rang and I sprang to my feet. I'd gone maybe five steps up the aisle when I realized that no one else was moving, not even to gather up their books and stuff. Everyone was sitting in their chairs, staring at me. No one was talking, not even Mr. Wilfred.

He smiled. "Going somewhere, Ms. Wakefield?" he asked.

I remembered his comment about the bells ringing every fifty minutes but class not being over, and my cheeks burned. I tried to think of some witty comment—some way to save the situation—but I couldn't. Now everyone thought I was a dork. A dork in a kilt. I turned and slunk back to my seat while everyone else laughed, Lacey harder than anyone.

Elizabeth

In my first class I'd sat with a girl I knew from SVMS, Ariel Childs, but in my second class, algebra, I didn't recognize anyone, so I slipped into a desk behind an Asian girl with beautiful long dark hair. She was talking to Salvador, the guy Brian had introduced me to.

"You promised to try out," the girl said.

I sat back and sneaked looks at Salvador. He had curly dark hair a shade lighter than the girl's and very mischievous eyes—he was the cutest guy I'd seen at junior high yet, but he was cute in an unusual way. It wasn't so much the way he looked, but the way he talked and moved.

"That was before I knew we'd be dealing with *her*," he said, nodding toward the front of the room.

I looked up and saw that a girl was talking to the teacher. The girl had very short, white blond hair and was wearing dark lipstick and fantastic horn-rimmed glasses that would have looked really gross on me. She was very tall and slender, and she wore leggings and a blue denim shirt. She looked incredibly cool in a way that I could never pull off.

"Salvador, you shouldn't let Charlie keep you from working on the *Spectator*," the girl said.

The *Spectator*! I looked back at the girl, Charlie, with even more interest. Was she the editor? I wished more than ever that I could be back at SVMS. If I were there, I'd be working on the paper; I probably would have been the editor this year. But I wasn't sure what my chances were of working on the *Spectator*. It's the best school paper in the county. Last year they even had an article written from the point of view of a dog. It really made you think about animal rights. I could never write anything that imaginative.

Salvador finally saw me and grinned. "Hi, Elizabeth!" he said, and the girl he had been talking to turned around and looked at me. I opened my mouth to reply but was interrupted.

"Could I have your attention, everyone?" said the teacher, Ms. Upton. "Before we start class, Charlie is here to talk to you about the *Spectator*. The floor is yours, Madame Editor."

Charlie stepped forward. She was so poised. I can never even give an oral report without shaking.

"Hi, everyone," Charlie said. Even her *voice* was

cool, low and throaty. "My name is Charmaine Roberts, and I'm editor of the *Spectator* this year. We have openings for five new staff members. I want to encourage only those people who are really serious about journalism to try out."

I couldn't believe you had to try out for the *Spectator.* At SVMS anyone who wanted to be on the papers was allowed to join. I thought of the SVMS papers with sudden embarrassment. What would Charlie Roberts think of them? Probably that they were incredibly babyish and stupid. And there were only five places open on the *Spectator.* I knew I wouldn't stand a chance, competing against all these students who knew Charlie, and the *Spectator,* and the school so much better than I did.

"Please raise your hand if you would like to try out," Charlie said. "I'll take your name and give you an application." She looked around expectantly.

A couple of people in the front row raised their hands, and Charlie took their names and handed them forms. The packets were really thick. *That's some application!* I thought. The girl in front of me raised her hand.

"Yes?" Charlie said.

"Anna Wang," the girl said.

Charlie walked down the aisle and handed Anna an application.

"Salvador del Valle," Salvador said. He grinned at Charlie, but she didn't smile back. She just wrote his name on her clipboard. *He's trying out?* I thought. Salvador seemed cool. And he was definitely cute. Maybe I *should* give it a shot. But what if I didn't make it?

"Anyone else?" Charlie asked. She looked around. "No more brave souls?" She shrugged. "Okay, then, thanks for your time. And good luck to everyone trying out."

She started walking up the aisle.

Suddenly I raised my hand. Ms. Upton saw me and nodded. "Yes?" she asked. "Do you need a bathroom pass?" I guess that was the only reason she could think of that I'd be raising my hand.

"No," I said, flashing a sideways glance at Salvador. My cheeks were burning, but he wasn't laughing, thank goodness. "I want to try out for the paper."

Jessica

"Okay, everyone, just take a seat on the benches against the wall." Miss Scarlett's eyes flicked over the group. "Guys on one side and girls on the other." I don't know why she added that part because no girls were sitting anywhere near the guys anyway.

I looked around for Lacey. I hadn't had any luck talking to her yet—in fact, I hadn't had much luck talking to *anybody* yet. It was starting to get a little frustrating. I mean, what do you say to people you've never met? "Hi, nice notebook"?

Lacey was already sitting on the bench with a girl on either side of her, so I sat next to the girl on her left, Kristin Seltzer. I've only been at junior high for half a day, and I already knew who Kristin Seltzer was because every single person she passes says hi to her. She's chubby, with an absolutely beautiful face and dazzling smile. Her hair is an unbelievable cloud of dark blond curls.

"I'm going to pass out the boys' swimsuits

first," Miss Scarlett said. "These are yours to keep—please inform your parents that they will receive a bill for them in the coming weeks. You will each get two suits to last you the whole marking period, so you'll need to take them home and wash them after each class." She walked down to the guys' end of the bench.

"Swimsuits?" I said, alarmed. "On my schedule it just says phys ed."

Kristin smiled at me. "Everyone has to take swimming for one marking period," she said.

"You're kidding." I groaned.

She shook her head. "I *wish* I were kidding."

Now, clearly this raised a serious problem, and Lacey and I said it at the same time: *"What will my hair look like?"*

"Jinx," Kristin said, laughing.

Lacey didn't look amused.

"You know," I said, wanting to keep this conversation going. "My friend Lila Fowler used to say that swimming was the absolute worst thing for your hair."

Now Lacey looked irritated, and I was afraid she was going to tell me to be quiet, but just then Kristin said, "Lila Fowler? You know her?"

"Sure," I said. "She's my best friend."

"Do *you* know her?" Lacey asked Kristin.

"Yeah, she's a cheerleader," Kristin said, and

35

Jessica

something in her voice made Lacey look at me with more interest.

A little flower of hope bloomed in my heart.

"Lila is my best friend," I repeated. "I just spent all yesterday shopping with her and—"

"Excuse me, girl in the purple plaid," Miss Scarlett interrupted. "Do you have something to share with the class?"

"No," I murmured, flushing.

I hate it when teachers don't bother to learn your name and refer to everyone by what they're wearing. Miss Scarlett sure knew how to work one's nerves.

"Now, I'll pass out the girls' suits in a minute," Miss Scarlett said. "But first I want to say a few words about hygiene. I'd like you all to wear flip-flops in the shower to prevent the spread of verrucas, more commonly known as plantar's warts."

Miss Scarlett yammered on about plantar's warts and athlete's foot, but I wasn't paying attention. I was too busy thinking about the fact that Kristin knew Lila. Knew her and liked her, apparently. It made sense—Lila had been my ticket to the SVMS in crowd. Clearly she was my ticket here too.

The bell finally rang and Miss Scarlett let us go to lunch, not that I had much appetite after all that talk about various fungi. I hoped that

Lacey or Kristin would invite me to join them, but Lacey only said, "Later," and wandered off. I decided against trailing after her. I didn't want to look like some desperate loser. Besides, I wanted to hang with Elizabeth at lunch. We couldn't really compare notes and gossip if Lacey and Kristin were at our table.

I went to the cafeteria and got in line. The food, as luck would have it, is the only thing that's the same here as it was at SVMS. Which is to say, nauseating. I decided to pack my own lunch tomorrow.

So I got my tray of globby mac and cheese and Jell-O and started looking for Elizabeth. I couldn't wait to find out if she had swimming too. I scanned the front of the cafeteria for her. Then I scanned the back. Then I scanned the middle. Then the whole thing over again.

My heart sank. Elizabeth wasn't there. She must have first lunch. I couldn't believe it. How could they not let twins have lunch together? Who did they expect me to eat lunch with?

I realized suddenly that that was a very good question. Who *was* I going to eat with?

This might sound babyish, but I really thought I might start crying. I absolutely couldn't let that happen in the middle of the lunchroom, so I took a couple of deep breaths and started moving.

Jessica

I walked slowly around the cafeteria, trying to keep a slightly bemused expression on my face, as if I were just having a little trouble finding my friends. It wasn't as if every table were totally full. Almost all of them had one or two empty chairs. But what would I say if I sat down with a bunch of people I didn't know? "Hi, I don't have any friends—do you mind if I sit with you?"

I saw Sally and Deena sitting together and began walking faster, not wanting them to see me. I certainly wasn't about to go for a repeat of this morning's scene in algebra in front of the entire student body.

Finally I spotted my locker partner, Ronald, at a table by himself, eating a sandwich and reading a paperback in a sort of bug-eyed way.

For a minute I almost doubled back. But where would I go? Could I possibly go through the lunch line again, pretending I wanted to exchange my Jell-O for pudding? *No*, I decided, *that would probably just make me look insane.*

Sit with a geek or by myself? I wondered. I reasoned that sitting with someone—no matter who it was—was less conspicuous than sitting by myself.

I swallowed hard as I went over and slammed my tray down across from Ronald. I guess it was the first time anyone had ever eaten lunch with him because he practically choked on his sandwich in surprise.

"Hi, Jessica," he said, after coughing a little. I tried to smile at him, but it came out more like a glare. I never would have been caught dead eating with this guy at SVMS, let me tell you. We sat in silence for a moment.

"Can I tell you something?" he asked finally.

"I guess so," I said.

"I really like your plaid skirt." Ronald smiled shyly.

That's when I vowed to burn the dumb thing in the backyard as soon as I got home.

Elizabeth

My gym locker happened to be right next to Anna Wang's, which made sense alphabetically. As we stood by our lockers, waiting for Miss Scarlett to pass out our uniforms, I wanted to say something to Anna, but I couldn't think of anything witty. Still, it seemed silly not to talk to her—she was in all of my classes and she knew Salvador. Besides, I was sick of not having anybody to talk to. So far nobody had been mean to me, but I was starting to feel as if I were invisible, drifting silently from class to class. I'd lucked out and eaten lunch with Susie Williams—another displaced SVMSer—but I hadn't seen Jessica all day.

I was desperately trying to think of something interesting to say to Anna when Miss Scarlett turned to me. "What size are you?"

"Um, medium, I guess," I said.

Miss Scarlett tossed me a blue uniform.

"Anna?" she asked.

"Small," Anna said.

"These are yours to keep," Miss Scarlett said. "Please inform your parents that they will receive a bill for them in the coming weeks. You will each get two uniforms to last you the whole marking period, so you'll need to take them home and wash them after each class."

The uniform was a hideous, navy blue polyester. I don't know why Miss Scarlett was even asking people what size they thought they were because the uniforms only come in gigantic or newborn. Mine was of the gigantic variety.

With a sigh I changed into my uniform, then turned to Anna. She had one of the newborn sizes—her top was skintight.

We looked at each other and shrugged. I smiled, but before I could see if Anna would smile back, Miss Scarlett clapped.

"Okay, girls," she said. "Let's get a move on. Come on out and line up on the bench."

We trooped out of the locker room and sat along a wooden bench that ran the length of the gym.

"All right," Miss Scarlett said. "First of all, I'd like to go over a few basic hygiene matters. Locker rooms are the perfect environment for many fungi and viruses—" She broke off suddenly, frowning. "Anna Wang, where is your sports bra?"

Oh. My.

I can't even describe how horrible that moment was. All the guys instantly leaned forward and stared at Anna's chest, which was only too clearly outlined in the navy blue polyester. I wanted to kill Miss Scarlett, and this wasn't even happening to me.

Anna crossed her arms over her chest. "I dropped it."

All the guys were grinning—except Salvador, who was glaring at Miss Scarlett. Even the girls were elbowing each other and smiling.

"You dropped your bra?" Miss Scarlett asked.

"Yes," Anna said. Her face was red, but her voice was firm. "In a puddle of water on the locker-room floor. You—you always say we shouldn't wear wet underwear."

Miss Scarlett looked absurdly pleased. "That's very true, Anna. Nothing is a better breeding ground for bacteria than wet underwear. But you simply can't attend gym class without a sports bra, because you are—"

I didn't know exactly what Miss Scarlett was going to say, but I guessed it would be something like "developing breasts," and if she said that, then all the whispers and giggles would erupt into laughter. It was all so awful. Anna cringed. I was amazed that she didn't start crying.

"I have an extra sports bra in my locker," I said suddenly. The words just came out on their own. "Anna can borrow it."

Anna gave me a quick look.

"Excellent," Miss Scarlett said. "Because a girl like Anna—"

"Miss Scarlett!" Salvador said urgently. "My toes itch!"

The color drained from Miss Scarlett's face. "Socks off, everyone!" she snapped. "I'm going to have to inspect feet. I might have known you'd show up with athlete's foot on the very first day of school, Salvador."

Everyone sighed and began untying their shoes.

"Should I take Anna back to my locker?" I asked.

"Oh yes, please," Miss Scarlett said distractedly.

I stood up and walked back into the locker room with Anna following.

"Thanks," she said softly as soon as we were out of earshot.

"It's no problem." I shook my head. Just thinking about the whole scene again made me a little nauseated and light-headed. I could only imagine how Anna was feeling.

Anna sighed. "I guess you know I didn't really drop my bra."

Elizabeth

"Well, I don't really have an extra one in my locker," I confessed.

I tried to imagine what we were going to tell Miss Scarlett when we walked back out without a bra. I couldn't. And I wasn't about to let Anna get humiliated again. I took a breath and said, "You know, we—we could buy you a bra."

She looked at me.

"We could go shopping," I explained.

Anna smiled a little. "Right now?"

"Sure," I told her, as if it were no big deal. "We could skip class. It's last period anyway, and Miss Scarlett won't notice. She's too busy checking feet." *Even if she does notice,* I thought, *I don't care.* And I really didn't—I was *furious* with Miss Scarlett at that moment.

Still, I don't know where that idea came from because I have never skipped class in my entire life. I've never skipped a pep rally, or an assembly, or a recess, even.

But Anna just said, "Okay. Let's go."

A n n a

The new girl and I left the school by the south doors so we'd have less chance of being seen.

I'd only skipped school a couple of times, always with Salvador, naturally. Once he'd heard that they were shooting a movie downtown, so we cut class to go, but it turned out that they were filming a documentary about traffic patterns. Story of my life.

"The mall's just a few blocks away," I said to the new girl. "I think they have an . . . underwear store there."

I said "I think" like I hadn't thought about going into House of Lingerie about a million times.

"My name is Elizabeth," the new girl said suddenly.

"I know." I laughed. "You're in all my classes. You probably know I'm Anna."

Elizabeth smiled too. She was taller than me

and really, really pretty, with long blond hair, bright blue-green eyes, and a great smile. And, of course, I owed her my life.

"Have you ever been bra shopping before?" I asked her. "I mean, by yourself?"

Elizabeth shook her head. "My mom always takes my sister and me," she said.

I sighed. My mom should have taken me a long time ago, but ever since Tim it's sometimes hard to talk to her. She has good days and bad days, and I never want to ruin one of the good days by asking her to take me shopping. Especially for a bra. And on the bad days, well . . . Of course, I could have gone by myself, but I kept putting it off. Maybe if I had a close friend who was a girl . . . But imagine if I'd recruited Salvador! Talk about humiliation.

"I can't believe Miss Scarlett asked you why you weren't wearing a bra," Elizabeth said suddenly.

"Wasn't it horrible?" I said.

"One time my mom asked me in front of my dad and brother if I had cramps," Elizabeth put in. "I thought I was going to die—and my brother nearly passed out."

"I know, my brother would have been the same way," I told her without thinking. When I realized what I'd just said, I felt like kicking myself. *Anna, you idiot, why'd you say that?* I glanced quickly at Elizabeth, but she didn't seem to think I'd said anything weird, which I guess I hadn't, unless you knew the situation.

We stopped walking. We were in front of the mall.

"Come on," Elizabeth said brightly. "How hard can it be?"

Answer: pretty hard.

First of all, when we walked in, the saleswoman behind the counter looked at us as though we were crashing her dinner party. "Can I help you?" she asked, but I could tell she really meant, *Get out.*

"No, thank you," Elizabeth said softly. "We're just browsing."

"Yeah," I added, just to let the saleswoman know she couldn't intimidate us.

So we browsed. We walked all the way around the store in a slow circle and stopped right in front of the bra section.

"Wow, Anna, these are expensive," Elizabeth whispered, looking at a price tag. "How much money do you have? I've only got ten dollars."

"I can put it on my mom's credit card," I told her. My mom lets me do a lot of my own shopping ever since Tim. But I was blown away that Elizabeth was willing to contribute to my first bra. She was pretty cool.

"Girls, did you come in here just to whisper and giggle?" the saleswoman asked.

Yes, we did, actually, I wanted to say. If I were with Salvador, I *would* have said it—but only if he didn't say it first. Somehow, though, I didn't want to sound like a total witch in front of Elizabeth, so we just sort of looked at each other uneasily.

Elizabeth lifted her chin. "We'd like to try on some bras," she said, and her voice only wavered a tiny bit on the *b*-word.

"Fine," the woman said. "What size? Is it for you?"

"It's for me," I said.

The woman stared right at my chest, and I had a horrible moment when I thought she was going to say something like, *About time, isn't it?* but she just plucked a bra off the rack and said, "This is a popular one among girls your age. And I think this would be your size."

"I need a sports bra too," I told her, and she picked one out and handed it to me without another word.

I thanked her, blushing, and Elizabeth and I took the bras off to the fitting room. I stepped into one of the stalls while Elizabeth waited right outside.

"That lady is awfully rude," Elizabeth whispered through the door.

"No kidding," I replied, unbuttoning my shirt.

Suddenly I felt really weird. This whole day was feeling somewhat unreal. I mean, who was this Elizabeth girl anyway? It had been stupid to bring someone I hardly knew bra shopping. It was just double the humiliation. *Oh, well,* I thought. *It could be worse. At least she's a girl; I could be here with someone like Salva—*

"Excuse me, ma'am." A familiar voice rang out from the sales floor. "But could you tell me something I've always wanted to know about training bras? How does the actual 'training' work?"

Talk about nightmares coming true.

Salvador was in the House. The House of Lingerie.

Elizabeth

"Young man," the saleswoman was saying when Anna and I emerged from the dressing room, "this is not an information desk. I don't have time to answer your mindless questions."

"Well, I wouldn't say it's a mindless question," Salvador said, leaning against the counter. "Otherwise you'd know the answer to it, right?"

"Are you here to shop for lingerie or not?" she asked huffily as Anna and I approached the counter. "Because I'm waiting on these two young ladies." I found that comment pretty ironic since she hadn't been too eager to wait on us five minutes ago.

"Yes, I'm actually here to buy a brassiere," Salvador said. His voice didn't waver at all, like mine had before. In fact, he pronounced *brassiere* with three syllables. I have to admit, I was kind of in awe of his courage. I don't usually enjoy watching someone acting rude, but

50

this particular saleswoman was getting exactly what she deserved.

The saleswoman raised an eyebrow. "You are?"

"Yes," Salvador said. "For my grandmother."

"How did you make out, dear?" the saleswoman asked, turning to Anna.

"These fit great," Anna replied. "Thank you *so much* for all the help," she added sarcastically. Anna fished her credit card and letter of permission to use it out of her bag and put them on the counter next to the bras.

"In fact," Salvador said, "I think my grandmother is about your size." He stared directly at the saleswoman's chest, and I let out a choking noise that I hoped didn't sound like the laugh it was.

"Young man!" the saleswoman said sternly. "Don't be rude."

The saleswoman turned her back to him, but she was so flustered that she had trouble putting Anna's mother's credit card through the machine. "Thank you, *girls*," she said pointedly.

"One more thing," Salvador said. He was still leaning against the counter. "What's a zebra?"

"A zebra?" the woman said. "What—"

"The largest size!" Salvador said, and cackled. "Get it?"

Okay, by now he was pretty over the top—but it

was still really hard to keep from laughing. Anna felt the same way; I could tell just by looking at her face. We each grabbed Salvador by the arm.

"Get it?" Salvador yelled as we dragged him out of the shop. "The largest size!"

Out in the hall, we could finally let out our pent-up laughter. I laughed until tears were streaming down my cheeks. Anna could hardly breathe.

"Oh, Salvador," Anna said, finally recovering her breath. "I don't know whether to thank you or kill you."

"Hey," Salvador protested. "You two abandoned me after I'd been totally heroic and pretended to have athlete's foot. Miss Scarlett wants me to go see a doctor!"

"Well, do you have athlete's foot?" Anna asked.

"No, Miss Scarlett has a phobia," Salvador said.

"How did you know where to find us?" I asked, wiping the tears from my face.

He smiled. "I asked for a bathroom pass and followed you. I was going to wait outside the store, but you were gone so long that I felt it was my duty to come in after you. Now, can we do something fun, like get a pizza? I'm starving."

"Sure," Anna said.

I suddenly felt awkward. Anna and Salvador

were clearly best friends. I couldn't tell whether I was invited to have pizza with them, so I somehow guessed not. "Well, see you tomorrow," I said.

"Aren't you coming?" Salvador seemed puzzled.

"Elizabeth," Anna said, taking my arm. "You have to come. This is a celebration pizza. For you and Salvador for saving me untold embarrassment."

"Yeah, Elizabeth." Salvador pretended to beg. "Please come."

"Well, okay," I agreed. "Just let me call my parents. And I have to be home by six—for dinner!"

"We'll put you on a bus with plenty of time to spare," Anna said. "But I can't promise you'll be hungry again."

So the three of us walked over to a restaurant called Vito's Pizza. It was a really nice place, with wood paneling and lots of plants—and a heavenly smell. We sat in a booth with really high seats, so that it seemed like we were the only three people in the restaurant. We ordered sodas and a pepperoni pizza, and while we were waiting, Salvador sat back and said, "Okay, let's list all of the bad things about Charlie Roberts."

"Top five or top ten?" Anna wanted to know.

Elizabeth

This must be a game they had played many, many times.

"Oh, top ten," Salvador said. He pulled a pencil stub out of his pocket and began writing on a paper napkin. "Number one. She looked soooo pleased when Ms. Upton called her Madame Editor."

"And she calls the journalism teacher Jerry instead of Mr. Desmond, like they're equals," Anna said.

"Oh yeah," Salvador said, writing. "And she sometimes refers to herself in the third person."

"She does?" Anna asked.

Salvador nodded. "She'll say, 'Charlie writes the editorials,' or whatever."

"Also," I said suddenly, "I'll bet those horn-rims have clear glass in them, not prescription lenses."

Salvador and Anna looked at me for a second and then burst out laughing.

"Good one." Salvador added it to his list.

That made me feel really happy, although I guess you probably shouldn't get a good feeling from saying bad things about someone.

But still, I have to admit it was fun. And when they put me on the bus later, Salvador and Anna stood on the corner and waved until they were out of sight. It occurred to me that I had done more than meet new people on the first day of junior high—I had made friends.

Jessica

"Um, excuse me," I said at dinner. "But does anyone care how *my* day was?"

"Don't interrupt, sweetie," my mother said automatically.

"I have to interrupt," I protested. "Steven has been talking about cars and Elizabeth has been talking about Anna and El Salvador until I—"

"Salvador, not El Salvador," Elizabeth said. (She has no sense of humor sometimes.)

"Doesn't anyone care about me?" I asked. "Go ahead, ask me how my day was."

"Okay," my dad said good-humoredly. "How was your day?"

"Horrible," I said. "I don't want to talk about it."

My dad rolled his eyes.

"I'm just kidding, Dad," I said. "Although my day was pretty horrible."

"What was so horrible about it?" my mom wanted to know. She looked concerned. "Didn't you make any new friends?"

"Sort of," I lied, shoving food around on my plate. Not wanting to go on about what an idiot I'd looked like all day and how it would be a miracle if anyone ever wanted to talk to me, I changed the subject. "My locker partner is the world's biggest nerd."

"Jessica," my dad said, "you shouldn't stereotype people like that."

"Dad." I pointed my fork at him. "This kid is building a ham radio in his basement out of old toaster parts. Need I say more? Lizzie, of course, got an incredibly cute locker partner," I added, glaring at her.

My father didn't look satisfied. "I just—"

The phone rang. "I'll get it," I said, pushing back my chair. "I'll let you know if it's El Salvador," I called over my shoulder to Elizabeth. She made a face.

I picked up the phone in the hall. It was Lila.

"Hey," I said. "I was going to call you after dinner. I met someone who knows you."

"Really? Who?"

"Kristin Seltzer."

"Oh," she said, sounding disappointed. "A girl."

"Well, yes," I said.

There was a pause.

"Do you know her?" I asked.

"I'm thinking," Lila said. "I can't really re-member. Anyway, how was the new school?"

"Well . . ." I hesitated.

"My day was great!" Lila burst out. I guess my hesitation was all the encouragement she needed. "We have this new teacher for homeroom, and he says that he's going to bring in doughnuts every morning until someone gets a detention."

"That's bribery," I said.

"Of course it is," Lila said cheerfully. "Even the teacher said so. But who cares? It's doughnuts."

"Doughnuts make you fat," I reminded her, which wasn't very nice, but I couldn't help myself.

I don't think Lila even heard me, though. "The cafeteria has a salad bar now, which was kind of cool but also kind of gross because some people were using their fingers instead of the salad tongs and sticking their heads under the sneeze guard."

"Well, at the junior high—," I started.

"And there's a new teacher who spits when he talks, and everyone's competing for the seats in the back rows," Lila continued. "I nearly got stuck up front, but this cute new guy offered me his seat, so now I'm in the very last row right next to Ellen."

"You're so lucky," I said weakly. I could hear the smile in her voice. What a great day Lila had had!

Jessica

Just hearing that she got to sit next to Ellen Riteman, one of my closest friends, made me jealous. I wanted to be happy for her, but it was hard.

"I know it."

"What did everyone say about your outfit?" I asked, remembering Lacey's smirk.

"What outfit?"

"The *Seventeen* outfit," I said, exasperated. Was she kidding? "The one we spent all day yesterday shopping for."

"Oh," Lila said absently. "I didn't wear it."

"You *what?*"

"I didn't wear it," she repeated. "I got up this morning and the purple plaid seemed really bright. It still has the tags on, so I'm going to return it."

"Well, mine doesn't," I said angrily. "Although it does have an applesauce stain. Listen, Lila, if you weren't going to wear yours, you should've called and told me."

"Why?" Lila said. "It's a free country. You can make up your own mind about what to wear."

"Yes, but the whole point was that we would be wearing the same thing!" I said, frustrated. I couldn't believe her. I'd at least wanted to hear that Lila had endured the same humiliation I had or else that everyone at SVMS had loved the outfit and the people at the junior high just didn't know good taste when they saw it—or *something*. I didn't want to think I'd gone through this all alone.

"Well, sorry," Lila said, sounding like she didn't know why I was upset. "It started to seem a little babyish to want to dress the same as my best friend. I mean, you and Elizabeth haven't done that since elementary school. Anyway, you should have been there today. It was really fun."

"Yeah, I guess." I sighed.

"So do you want to come over after school tomorrow or something?" Lila asked.

I felt a little better. "Yeah," I said. "Sounds good." I was dying to see someone I was actually friends with. I mean, I was trying to keep my chin up and look on the bright side—I'd have another chance to meet people tomorrow—but it was hard. My first day of junior high had been one of the worst days of my life.

"Great," Lila said, and we said good-bye and hung up.

It wasn't until later that I realized Lila had said, "You should have been there." Which, when you think about it, was not quite the same as saying, "I missed you."

Salvador

I met the Doña coming up the drive, carrying a bag of groceries. "Hi," I said. "Let me carry those."

The Doña is my grandmother. I gave her the nickname after a character on some old Western I saw on television. I know she loves it when I call her that, no matter how much she denies it.

"Hello, Salvador," she said, handing me the bag of groceries. "How does chicken teriyaki sound for supper?"

"Great." I patted my stomach. "I'm starved." I'd just eaten half a pepperoni pizza, but I was still hungry. Besides, the Doña took a Japanese cooking class last year, and her chicken teriyaki is fantastic.

"Well, good, because I need a prep chef," the Doña said.

We went into the kitchen, and I began unpacking the groceries while the Doña played back the messages on our answering machine.

There was a message from my mom: "Hi, sweetie, I'm just calling to see how your first day of school went, but I guess you're not there. Talk to you later. I love you."

I've lived with the Doña since the fifth grade because both my parents are in the military and they move around a lot. One Christmas the Doña started talking about how much she loves company, and I started talking about how much I hated to move, and the whole family decided it would solve a lot of problems if I just stayed here. Lots of people would hate my situation. For example, I could never live with my *other* grandmother. Once when I was staying with her, I woke up in the middle of the night and she was holding a mirror under my nose to make sure I was still breathing!

The Doña is nothing like that, and I love staying with her. My cousin Mark dug it too when he stayed here with us last month. We live in this giant house that my grandmother says is much too big for two people, so she's always inviting other people over.

"So how was the first day of school?" she asked, putting some carrots on the cutting board in front of me.

"Fine," I replied.

"I want you to know that I'm very proud of

you," the Doña said, "for getting through the first day of school without the principal calling. I think it's a record."

"Don't exaggerate." I pointed a carrot at her. "Did the principal call on the first day of school last year?"

"Yes," the Doña said unblinkingly.

"Well, didn't it turn out to be a huge misunderstanding?" I asked. Someone had drawn a caricature of Mrs. Pomfrey on her chalkboard, and she assumed it was me because I did the same thing last year. But I had an ironclad alibi.

"Well, let's hope we don't have any more misunderstandings." The Doña got out another cutting board and began trimming the fat off the chicken. "So, talk to me. Tell me the best thing about the first day of school."

"That's easy," I said. "Elizabeth Wakefield."

From Elizabeth Wakefield's
Spectator Application:

3. If you were the editor (which you're not, obviously), what would you change about the *Spectator*?

I would do more interviews with just "average" students because I think everyone has something extraordinary about him or her.

4. What do you feel you have to offer the *Spectator*?

I'm a good communicator and a hard worker. I have previous newspaper experience and would be happy to undertake any assignments, no matter how menial.

5. Are you a reliable person?

Yes, extremely.

6. How many late days did you have last year?

Ten, but that is because my sister absolutely cannot understand that if she plugs in the blow-dryer while the dishwasher is running, it blows a fuse and then we all have to scurry around in the dark, trying to get things started again.

Jessica

The very first thing Ronald Rheece said to me when I got to my locker on the second day of school was, "Jessica, I can't have lunch with you today because of chess-club tryouts."

"Chess club?" I asked. "You have to try out? I thought you'd be a shoo-in."

Ronald got that proud look again. "Well, the coach did say it was basically a formality and—"

"Anyway," I said, poking him in the chest. "We did not *have lunch* together yesterday because that would require some sort of conversation other than you telling me about your stupid ham radio."

"You asked!" Ronald squeaked. "You said, 'What's new, Ronald?' and I said, 'I'm building a ham radio—'"

I rolled my eyes. Did he have to recite the whole conversation? It hadn't been that great the first time we had it.

"Okay, Ronald," I interrupted. "Thanks for the

64

warning about lunch." I decided against telling him that I never wanted to have lunch with him in public again and patted him on the shoulder instead. "Good luck."

He smiled, and I grabbed my bag and headed toward the exit.

Thank goodness I got out of that one, I thought. I really didn't want to further my friendship with Ronald and become a nerd by association.

Anyway, I was on a mission. Today I would sit with the cool people. After all, I was one of them.

But I hadn't managed to talk to Lacey, or Kristin, or anyone else by the time swimming class rolled around. I put on the ugly black swimsuit and shoved my hair into a bathing cap. It felt like a giant leech on my head.

Miss Scarlett lined the class up on the bench again.

"Now, girls," she said, "I don't allow anyone who is having her period to go swimming. It's extremely unsanitary. Are any of you menstruating?"

I gasped. Did Miss Scarlett actually mean that if you have your period, you have to announce it in front of *the whole class?* I was mortified enough just by her *question*—but I couldn't even imagine having to *answer* it.

Jessica

The guys quieted right down and their eyes got all glittery. I know they were just dying for some poor girl to raise her hand so they could make her miserable for the rest of her life. Luckily no one did.

I never will, that's for sure. I don't care if I have to lie to Miss Scarlett or fake the flu and stay home from school. I will never raise my hand and say, *Yes, Miss Scarlett, I* am *menstruating!* I started blushing just thinking about it, and I desperately hoped that nobody was seeing me blush and thinking that I was getting my period right at that moment and my face was turning red because I was keeping quiet about it. I peered around at the other girls to see if anyone was looking at me, but they were just staring at their feet.

Looking at them, I was suddenly furious with Miss Scarlett. What was her deal anyway? I'd never heard that going swimming with your period was unsanitary. In fact, we'd seen a video last year that said you could do anything, including swimming, when you have your period. If you ask me, Miss Scarlett is something of a nutcase.

I couldn't *wait* for this day to be over so I could go hang with Lila—by *her* pool, where I could wear whatever swimsuit I wanted and wouldn't have to worry about getting humiliated every second of the day.

"Okay," Miss Scarlett said. "I'm going to have you get into the pool, five at a time, so I can assess your swimming ability."

She called the first five names, and as soon as she was busy at the poolside, I slid down the bench to where Kristin and Lacey were talking. It was time to get moving on my mission.

"Hi," I said.

Kristin smiled, but Lacey looked a little annoyed.

"I spoke to Lila last night," I began.

"Who?" Lacey demanded.

"Lila Fowler," I said, feeling flustered. "Yesterday Kristin said she knew her."

"Oh yeah, that's right," Kristin said. "How is she?"

"She's fine," I said, feeling like an idiot. This conversation was *not* going according to plan. Why couldn't Kristin and Lacey remember me from yesterday and ask me something about myself? "I'm going over to her house this afternoon."

Lacey didn't look all that impressed by this piece of information, so I hurried on. "She lives in a mansion, and it's really incredible. Her pool is huge." I laughed. "And *her* bathing caps are way more stylish than these," I added sarcastically.

Lacey and Kristin exchanged glances.

"She wears a bathing cap in her own pool?" Lacey asked, arching one of her perfect eyebrows. Then she nudged Kristin. "She sounds *real* cool."

I felt the blood rush to my cheeks. What was the deal—didn't anyone at this stupid school understand *irony?* "N-No," I stammered. "I was only kidding. I mean, we don't really wear bathing caps. We wear, uh, regular stuff. You know, bikinis, flip-flops. . . ."

What were these words spewing out of my mouth? I didn't even have to look at Kristin and Lacey to know how idiotic I sounded. Somehow I didn't seem to have any control over what I was saying. I had this weird feeling, as if I were outside of my body, watching myself say dumb things, and I was powerless to stop it. At SVMS everyone knew who Lila Fowler was. Everyone wanted to be her friend. But I wasn't at SVMS. That was the whole problem. I had to get off the Lila kick.

"Do you like swimming?" I asked, tilting my rubber-encased head in what I hoped was a friendly, cool pose.

Kristin was looking at me in a puzzled way, and a tiny line had appeared between Lacey's dark eyebrows. I guess that question had sounded kind of random. And hadn't we discussed how much we didn't like swim class the day before? I suddenly felt embarrassed. Who knows how much longer we would have sat there staring at one another if Miss Scarlett hadn't called Kristin and Lacey to the pool?

"See you guys later," I said lamely.

"Bye," Kristin said. Lacey didn't say anything. And they didn't invite me to lunch—for obvious reasons.

Later, during my swimming assessment, Miss Scarlett said in this really loud voice, "Nice brrreaststroke, Jessica!" and trilled the *r* just like that.

So now about a million guys I don't even know keep coming up to me and saying, "Nice brrreaststroke, Jessica!" Which is three more words than any of them had said to me up until now, but I still feel like locking myself in my room and never coming out. I don't know what I would do if I weren't seeing Lila this afternoon.

From Salvador del Valle's
Spectator Application:

12. If you could "right" one of the world's "wrongs," which would it be?

I would make it so that there were more Crunchberries than plain cereal in Cap'n Crunch.

13. If you could put any one law into effect, what would it be?

I would make it illegal for women to take their grandsons shoe shopping with them. It would constitute child abuse.

14. Why do you think you are uniquely qualified to work for the *Spectator*?

I am by far the seediest person applying and would be good at undercover assignments.

A n n a

After school, Elizabeth, Salvador, and I handed our applications to Charlie, who was collecting them just outside the journalism room.

"Oh boy," Elizabeth said as we walked away. "Now I'm regretting every single thing I wrote down."

"Me too," I said. I felt like I would do anything to have that application back. I wished that I hadn't attached one of my poems at the back. Why was I so dead set on embarrassing myself lately?

I'd hated not making the paper last time. But my chances had to be better now, didn't they? I can't explain it, but my writing has become incredibly important to me over the last year. And for some reason, the idea of belonging to a group of people who liked to write really appealed to me. I've never been part of a crowd—I've just been best friends with Salvador since, well . . . forever. He hangs out with other people sometimes, but I don't usually join him when he does. I don't usually like hanging out with most of his guy friends—his cousin Mark being a prime example.

"Come on, you guys," Salvador said. "We're bound to make it." He didn't sound nervous, but I could tell he was. He always keeps his left hand in his pocket when he's worried about something.

We walked out of the building toward Elizabeth's bus.

"I'm not going to sleep at all tonight," Elizabeth confided.

I smiled at her. She was really nice. It was cool to have a girlfriend—it was different. I had started to say something when a guy I didn't know walked past and said, "Nice brrreast-stroke!" All his friends laughed.

Elizabeth and I looked at each other. "What did that mean?" Elizabeth asked me.

"I don't know." I turned to Salvador, who was on my other side. "What did it mean?"

"How would I know?" Salvador protested.

"You're a guy," I said.

"Yeah," Elizabeth echoed. "Translate."

Salvador rolled his eyes. "Listen, you probably don't want to know what it meant."

"True," Elizabeth said, sighing.

Salvador smiled at her. "I'm sure in your case, it was a compliment, though."

In her *case!* I thought indignantly.

Elizabeth laughed. "You think so?" She looked skeptical.

"Sure," Salvador said. "You're so—"

"Could we skip the chest remarks today?" I said crossly. "I had enough of that yesterday."

Elizabeth and Salvador looked up, startled. "I didn't mean that—," Salvador began.

"Sorry," I cut him off again, flushing.

"It's okay," Elizabeth said with a smile.

Salvador just gave me a look, and I shrugged. I wondered what he had been about to say. You're so . . . what?

For no reason at all, I remembered this one day I'd gone downtown to meet Salvador at the movie theater. As I walked up, he gave a big wolf whistle. I was really pleased because I was wearing a new skirt, and he doesn't usually notice stuff like that. But as soon as I came up to him, he said, "I know you think whistling is the lowest form of compliment, but I couldn't help it. Darla Simmons is so gorgeous!" I turned around, and sure enough, Darla looked incredible in her high-topped boots and skirt—*which happened to be the exact same one as mine.*

I felt now exactly what I'd felt then.

We crossed the lawn in front of the school to where Elizabeth's sister was waiting by the bus. I hadn't met Jessica before, but it wasn't hard to figure out who she was.

Elizabeth introduced everyone.

"Hi, Jessica," I said. "Wow, Elizabeth, I didn't know you were a twin!"

"Hey, I know you," Salvador said to Jessica. "You're the girl who wore a purple blanket yesterday."

Jessica gave him a sour look. "It's nice to meet you too, El Salvador," she said.

I rolled my eyes and exchanged a look with Elizabeth. Clearly her sister and Salvador were hardly a match made in heaven.

I was still getting over how identical Elizabeth and Jessica were. I mean, obviously they're twins, but it was almost uncanny. I decided that Jessica was actually prettier than Elizabeth, but maybe that's because her eyes were so bright and her cheeks were flushed.

Suddenly a whole group of guys stopped before getting on the bus. "Nice brrreaststroke, Jessica!" one of them yelled. All the guys cracked up.

"Shut up," she said hotly.

"What does that mean?" Elizabeth asked her sister.

"It's a long story and I don't want to talk

about it." Jessica threw back her shoulders. "Are you ready to go?"

"Sure," Elizabeth said. She turned to us. "Well, bye."

We waved, and she and her sister got on the bus. Salvador and I began walking home.

"Who do you think is prettier, Elizabeth or Jessica?" I wondered out loud.

I didn't really expect Salvador to answer because he usually avoids any conversation he thinks is "girly." But then he said, "Elizabeth. By far."

"Really?" I was surprised. "Why?"

He shrugged. "I just do."

That feeling I'd had started creeping over me, so I changed the subject. "Listen," I said, "what movie do you want to watch on Saturday night?" Salvador and I have watched videos together at my house on Saturdays for as long as I can remember.

"Well, it's your week to choose," he said, "but I'm warning you—no chick flicks."

"That's why I'm asking you," I said patiently.

He considered for a moment. "Something violent, then."

I rolled my eyes. Maybe next week I would invite Elizabeth to join us on Saturday night and we could outvote Salvador. But for some reason, I didn't want to do that this week. I wanted things to be just the two of us.

"Why don't you come in and we can look through the Doña's video guide?" Salvador asked as we drew near his big Tudor house.

"Sure," I said.

But as I followed him up the drive, I had a horrible thought. What if Salvador and Elizabeth made the paper and I didn't? That would be terrible. They would hang out together all the time. Oh, occasionally they'd still see me for old time's sake and they'd try not to talk about the paper too much. I would probably feel obligated to join some other pitiful club like Future Scientists of America and try to make it sound cool when I talked to Elizabeth and Salvador. Maybe I would have to hang out with Ronald Rheece and—

"What are you doing?" Salvador asked.

I started. "What?"

"What are you doing?" he repeated. "You're standing totally still, but your lips are moving."

"Oh, I—nothing." I tried to brush the whole ugly fantasy from my mind.

Salvador held the door open for me, and I hurried up the steps.

Stop being paranoid, I told myself sternly. Elizabeth and Salvador and I would go on being friends no matter what. I was sure of it.

I can be so stupid sometimes.

Jessica

"Do you want a snack?" Elizabeth asked as we let ourselves into the house.

"No, I'm going over to Lila's," I said. "So—"

The ringing phone cut me off. I picked it up in the kitchen. "Hello?"

"Jessica?" It was Lila. "I'm so glad I caught you."

"Hi," I said. "I'll be right over; I just wanted—"

"Wait," Lila said. "I'm not at home. I'm still at school. I forgot that today is Booster tryouts, and since I'm captain, I obviously have to be there. So I guess you'll have to come over another day."

I opened my mouth, but no sound came out. I stared at the phone as if had betrayed me.

"Jessica?" Lila asked. "Are you still there?"

"Yeah," I said, and my voice sounded perfectly normal. "We'll do it another day, no problem."

"Hold on a sec," Lila said. I could hear voices in the background and someone asking, "Who

77

are you talking to?" and Lila saying, "Jessica."

For a horrible moment I imagined that the person would say, *Jessica who?* and Lila would have to say, *Jessica Wakefield, remember?*

But instead the voice said, "Oh, tell her I said hi!"

"Ellen says hello," Lila said into the phone. "I'll be there in a minute," she said to Ellen. "Listen, I'm having a sleep over on Saturday," she told me. "You'll be there, right?"

And suddenly she seemed like the old Lila (that is, the Lila of two days ago), who was such good friends with me that she didn't even need to consult me.

"I'll be there," I said, making a mental note to ask my parents later.

"Great," Lila said. "We're all going to see *Cool Dudes* first. Can you have your dad drop you off at the Regency at seven o'clock?"

"Sure, I can hardly wait," I said truthfully. "See you then."

I hung up and went into the kitchen, where Elizabeth was spreading peanut butter on rice cakes.

"Can I have one?" I asked.

"I thought you were going to Lila's," she said, handing me one.

"Change of plans," I said. "So, do you want to watch TV?"

Elizabeth shook her head. "I have too much algebra homework." She looked at me curiously. "Don't you have any homework?"

"I already did it," I said.

"When?" Elizabeth asked.

"During French," I lied. I'd actually done it in the girls' bathroom during lunch. I'd eaten my ham sandwich there too, sitting on the radiator.

Elizabeth poured herself a glass of milk. "I'm going up to my room," she announced.

I sighed. Maybe I'd watch TV if there was anything decent on. At least I didn't have to study. It's funny how you get more schoolwork done when you don't have a busy social life. That's probably something Ronald Rheece knows a thing or two about.

Elizabeth

"You should have tried out for yearbook," Jessica told me on the bus the next morning.

"Why?" I asked.

"Because then you could make sure lots of pictures of me got in and it would look like I was really involved in things," Jessica said.

That struck me as a weird comment, especially coming from Jessica. Usually she looks like she's involved in things because she *is* involved in things. It was strange not having any classes together—I hardly knew what was going on with her. "You could join yearbook and do that for yourself," I suggested.

"Bo-ring," Jessica said, playing with the zipper on her backpack. "And too much work. Anyway, you can write me up for 'Notes on Newcomers' if you make the *Spec*."

"Okay," I said. I paused. "But seriously, Jess, you could join something. It would be a good way to meet people."

80

Jessica glared at me. "Now who's talking like Dad?" she snapped.

"Sorry," I said, and bit my lip.

Jessica slouched back in her seat. "Liz, do you ever wish we were still at SVMS?"

I thought about it. "Well . . . I miss Maria and Todd. And I wish that I were running the paper instead of trying out for it." I shrugged. "But I like junior high."

She sighed. "But we don't rule the school like we would have. You thought it was so unfair when we first found out."

"Well, yes," I said. "I did think it was unfair that your address could change your life, but—" I broke off, seeing Jessica's face. Her eyes had gotten very wide. "What's wrong?"

"Nothing," she said absently. "We're almost there."

"Jessica, is everything okay with you?"

She looked at me for a second. "Everything's fine, Lizzie," she said finally. "It looks like your friends are waiting for you."

I glanced up. Anna and Salvador were standing near the bus stop. At the sight of them my throat closed. I tried to tell by their faces if they knew who made the paper, but Anna looked as tense as I felt and Salvador just looked the same as always.

I wanted to make the paper in the worst way, and not only because I missed writing. I wanted to go on being friends with Anna and Salvador, and I knew it would be difficult if they made the paper and I didn't. They would be friends with each other because they had been for years, but how would it work if we didn't have the *Spectator* in common?

"Hi," I said as Jessica and I got off the bus. Jessica waved absentmindedly as she headed off to her locker. "Is the list up?" I asked Anna.

"It should be," she replied. Her voice was cracking. "You ready to go look?"

I took a breath. "Sure." I followed Anna and Salvador toward the door nearest the journalism room.

"I can't stand the suspense," Anna said suddenly.

"Me either," I said.

"Oh, come on." Salvador put an arm around each of us. "I bet you both have sweaty palms and armpits, and it's just not worth it."

"How can you joke about this?" Anna asked.

"Because I joke about everything," Salvador said. "I even put jokes on my application."

"You didn't!" Anna said. Then she looked at his face and moaned. "I take that back. I'm sure you did. I just hope it wasn't that zebra one."

I didn't say anything. I wished Salvador didn't have his arm around me because it made it difficult to concentrate.

And then we were right in front of the journalism room. *Jessica was right,* I thought in a panic. *We belong at SVMS, where I'd be running the paper and not feeling all queasy.*

A single sheet of white paper was taped to the journalism-room door. New *Spectator* Staff, it said at the top. Below that were typed five names. I could barely make myself read them.

Salvador del Valle
Ivy Hampton
Damon Ross
Elizabeth Wakefield
Anna Wang

I closed my eyes and willed my heart to stop hammering.

Anna let out a squeal and then suddenly stopped as a voice from behind us said, "Congratulations."

I opened my eyes and turned around. It was Charlie Roberts. She was wearing a white T-shirt with a zebra-striped scarf. Her lipstick was so dark, it was almost black.

"Thanks," I said weakly, happy that I hadn't started dancing around or doing anything stupid before she appeared.

Charlie smiled at all three of us. "So, listen, the first meeting is tonight at seven—you know

Elizabeth

that, right? Mr. Desmond drops by sometimes, but usually only when we're close to going to print. Meetings are always on Fridays," she went on, "but we usually order pizza, and most of the time everyone goes out together afterward, so it's not going to wreck anyone's social life."

"Cool," Salvador said.

A bell rang. "Well, I'd better go," Charlie said. She threw her zebra scarf over her shoulder and gave us a final dazzling smile. "See you tonight."

"See you," Anna said, and Salvador nodded. I couldn't help thinking that if we hadn't made the paper, Charlie wouldn't have smiled at us in a million years. In fact, she would never have acknowledged our existence.

I turned to Anna and Salvador to ask if they thought so too. But before I could say anything, Salvador put his arm around each of us again and began leading us back down the hall. I didn't mind his arm this time. It just felt natural.

Jessica

"Wakefield?" Miss Scarlett said. "Wakefield!"

I started. "What?"

"It's your turn for laps," Miss Scarlett said.

All the guys started grinning when she said that, but I barely paid attention. Ever since Elizabeth said that thing about your address changing your life, my brain had been working overtime.

What if I could use Lila's mailing address and still be eligible to go to Sweet Valley Middle School? I was sure Lila wouldn't mind. But what if I had to sleep there during the week? Mr. Fowler always said I was welcome anytime. . . .

I walked to the edge of the pool, tightened the strap on my bathing cap, and dove in. I slipped into a front crawl (I'm never doing the breaststroke again, believe me).

I can't wait to get back to SVMS, I thought as I sliced through the heavily chlorinated water. I was beginning to think that I'd never really appreciated my friends . . . back when I had friends.

After swimming, I went straight to the girls' bathroom at lunch hour. I brought my sandwich and my algebra textbook. At SVMS you had to have a hall pass if you weren't in the cafeteria at lunch. But here none of the teachers seemed to notice or care where you went.

When I pushed open the swinging door, I froze.

Lacey Frells was standing at one of the sinks with a lit cigarette in her hand.

Lacey looked a little worried when she saw me, but I just smiled and said, "Miss Scarlett would have a stroke if she caught you."

Lacey relaxed. "That would be a public service," she said, taking a puff of her cigarette.

"I know it," I said.

I got a brush out of my purse and began brushing my hair so I would have an excuse to stand at the sinks too.

Just then a girl came out of one of the stalls. "Hi, Elizabeth," she said to me.

I gave her a tense smile, not wanting to be interrupted while I was talking to Lacey. "I'm Jessica. You're thinking of my twin sister."

"Oh," the girl said. "Sorry." She washed her hands and left.

"You have a twin?" Lacey said. "That's cool."

I shrugged.

"Where's Kristin?" I asked casually.

"She has a cheerleader meeting," Lacey said. "They're getting together to discuss tryouts."

I had a sudden surge of hope. Maybe without Kristin around, Lacey would invite me to have lunch with her.

"Lila and I used to be cheerleaders at SVMS. In fact, she was at the tryouts last night," I said. "I mean, she didn't have to try out—she was actually there to judge the other girls. She called me, you know, right in the middle . . ."

Lacey jammed her curling iron into her bag. I knew I had to stop babbling.

"Why aren't you a cheerleader, Lacey?" I asked.

She looked me in the eye. "Because cheerleading's lame," she said icily, and turned to go.

I felt like someone had sucked all the air out of my lungs and couldn't think of any way to respond. "Bye," I said faintly, knowing she wasn't going to invite me to lunch now.

Lacey didn't even bother to respond. She just walked quickly out of the bathroom, her bag swaying against her hip.

I wiped away a tear that was trickling down my cheek. This change-of-address thing had better work.

Anna

At six-thirty I rang the bell at Salvador's house and the Doña let me in. "Hi, Mrs. del Valle," I said.

"Hello, Anna," she said, smiling. "Come on in. Salvador will just be a minute—he's upstairs changing."

Changing? I thought. *As in, clothes?* That was a little weird. Over the summer Salvador wore the same T-shirt for three straight months. I thought it had become part of his skin.

But the Doña didn't seem to think it was odd. "Let's have a cup of tea in the library," she suggested.

"Okay," I said.

We walked down a short hall. I don't think I'd like living in a house with so many rooms. Our house is about one-tenth the size of this, and sometimes *it* seems big and echoey. Plus the Doña's house has about a million antiques in it, and I would live in fear of breaking them. Though

88

Anna

actually, Salvador has broken quite a few and the
Doña never flies off the handle or anything.

The tea service was already set out on a low
table, and the Doña motioned for me to sit in
one of the library's overstuffed chairs.

"It's so nice to have someone to drink tea
with," she said, pouring. "Salvador can never sit
still long enough."

"Yes, he's like that," I agreed. I took the cup
she held out to me. Most people my age don't
drink tea. But I'm not like most people.

The Doña poured herself a cup and settled
back in her chair. She's really easy to talk to.

"Are you taking any classes right now?" I
asked, raising the steaming cup to my lips. She's
always taking classes.

"Yes, I have fencing tonight," the Doña said.
"The teacher said I'm the best student in his class."

"Do you have to wear a uniform?" I asked. I
always thought fencers wore all white, with a
mask, but the Doña was just dressed in a pow-
der blue sweat suit.

She laughed. "No, just in competition and I'm
not ready for that—yet. How are things with you?"

"Oh, fine," I said.

"You must be very excited about working on
the paper," the Doña said.

I nodded and took another sip. "Maybe I

89

could write a story about your fencing class."

Normally the Doña would jump all over an offer like that, but now she just regarded me with her bright eyes. "How are things at home?"

"Things at home are fine too," I said.

"Your mother is doing well?" the Doña asked.

I dropped my eyes. Sometimes I think the Doña suspects something about my mom and her bad days. I've never told anyone, not even Salvador, but every once in a while the Doña will say something and I get very scared.

"My mom's fine," I said, wondering how many times I could possibly use the word *fine* in this conversation.

The Doña opened her mouth to say something, but just then Salvador bounded into the room, knocking over a footstool. "Hi, Anna. I'm ready," he said, bending over to put it upright again.

He was wearing clean jeans and a shirt so new, I could still see the creases where it had been folded.

"Is that the shirt I gave you for Christmas?" the Doña asked in a pleased-sounding voice.

Salvador looked down. "Yeah."

"Well, you look very handsome," she said.

I stood up. "Thank you for the tea."

"Anytime, Anna," the Doña said. "It's a pleasure."

I followed Salvador out of the house, and we

began walking toward school. He was walking really fast.

"Relax," I said. "We have plenty of time."

"What?" Salvador asked.

"I said, we have plenty of time," I repeated.

"Oh yeah," he said. He slowed down for about two steps and then began hurrying again.

He must be really excited about this meeting, I thought. I wondered if that was why he was wearing a new shirt.

"Hey, slow down," I said.

Salvador was staring off into space. Was he even listening to me?

"So I thought tomorrow we could watch *The Little Mermaid*," I told him.

"Okay," Salvador said absently.

Now I knew he wasn't listening! He once said that *The Little Mermaid* was the most boring movie ever made.

"Can I borrow fifty bucks?" I asked.

"Sure."

"What's the capital of Florida?"

"All right."

I shook my head. "You are acting really bizarre."

"Okay," Salvador replied. He was miles away.

Jessica

After dinner I decided to call Lila to see if she wanted to get together. I thought maybe we could go shopping for party supplies or something, but I just got her answering machine.

Oh, well, I thought, hanging up without leaving a message. *I'll just see her tomorrow.* I went into the kitchen, where my mom was finishing the dishes. Steven hurried in after me.

"So I can borrow the car, Mom?" he asked.

"Yes," my mom said. "Have fun."

"Where are you going?" I asked Steven.

"Crazy," he said, and walked out the door, jingling the keys. Sometimes I wish Steven would, like, be adopted by another family or something.

My mom turned to face me. "Steven's going bowling with Joe Howell," she explained. "And what about you? Do you have any plans?"

"No," I said darkly, and went upstairs to

Elizabeth's room. "Hey," I said, knocking on her open door. "Want to go to a movie?"

"I can't," Elizabeth said, fastening an earring onto her right ear. "Anna and Salvador and I have a *Spec* meeting."

Did the whole world have plans except for me? "Why don't you three just have yourselves surgically attached and get it over with?" I asked crossly.

Elizabeth looked hurt. "Jessica, I'm sorry, but I can't skip the first meeting."

"Forget it," I said, flouncing out of her room. I didn't want Elizabeth feeling sorry for me. I could spend one Friday night at home, watching TV with my parents (even though my dad would probably want to watch some stupid ball game).

I went into my own room to pack my overnight bag for Lila's. I packed a clean nightgown and then a sweatshirt in case we went outside and another T-shirt in case we ordered pizza or something messy. I threw in some magazines and a new lipstick.

"Hey," my dad said from the doorway. "Is this a sleep over, or are you moving to Lila's permanently?"

Don't tempt me, I thought. But I didn't say anything because he's really awfully nice and it's not his fault that I don't want to live here anymore.

Elizabeth

"Hi," Charlie said as we arrived in the journalism room. "Just have a seat."

I'd met Anna and Salvador outside. We found chairs near one another at the front of the room and watched Charlie sort through her pile of folders.

Two more people came in and sat down, and Charlie took a brief head count. "Okay, everyone's here," she said, standing by Mr. Desmond's desk. "Welcome to this year's first meeting. Obviously most of you already know me from last year. This year we have five new minions, Ivy, Elizabeth, Damon, Salvador, and Anna. I'm sure you'll all get to know them."

I didn't know what *minion* meant, but I didn't like the sound of it. And I didn't like the way Charlie had only used our first names. I looked at the other two new people with interest. Ivy was petite, with strawberry blond hair and glasses. Damon had very short brown hair and looked really athletic, much more athletic than anyone else in the room.

Charlie continued, "Now, I want the paper to be really great this year, and I want everyone who works on it to come away with some journalistic experience. I mean that—I want each and every one of you to do some real investigative reporting. And I'm very, very interested in any new ideas that you might have."

One person started to raise his hand, and Charlie added, "I'm interested in hearing them *later.* All right," she went on, picking up the folders in front of her. "Tonight's business is advertising."

She walked down the aisle. "Anna," she said, putting a file on Anna's desk. "This is a list of photographers who advertised with us last year." Charlie looked at us. "Photographers are always a good bet because they think we'll use them when we need school pictures taken. Anyway, Anna, I want you to look through the yellow pages and see if you can find any new photographers we should contact. The phone book is in Mr. Desmond's desk drawer. You can sit up there."

Anna nodded and quickly scurried up to the front of the room.

"Elizabeth," Charlie said. She didn't give me a folder. "That box by the door contains back issues of the paper and envelopes addressed to last year's contributors. I need you to put the papers in the envelopes and mail them out so people can see where their money went. Salvador can help you."

Charlie continued down the aisle, giving assignments.

I gave Salvador a small what-can-you-do? smile and went to get the box. When I came back, he had pushed our desks together. We made a pile of papers and a pile of envelopes and got to work.

I tried to listen to what assignments the other staff members were getting, but I couldn't hear. A couple of people were busily reading folders, and Charlie was talking quietly with a group of about five or six in the back.

"Hey, look at Anna," Salvador said suddenly, grinning. "She looks like she's actually reading the phone book."

I glanced over and laughed because that was exactly what Anna did look like, bent over the phone book, studiously examining every page before she turned to the next one. Anna heard me and looked up, puzzled.

I shook my head at her, mouthing, "I'll tell you later." She frowned a little bit and went back to work.

There must have been about a thousand envelopes in that box, and I'm not exaggerating.

Salvador and I worked hard for over an hour and the box was still half full.

"Wow," Salvador said, "this fast-paced investigative-reporter life is getting to me. Paper cuts and paste poisoning are major occupational hazards."

I giggled.

"Seriously," he protested. "I could bleed to death from a cut on my tongue before they could get my mouth unstuck. Charlie would probably write a story about it. 'Youth Perishes While Paramedics Labor to Unfasten Lips.'"

I laughed, stopping when I noticed Salvador was staring at me. "What is it?" I said.

He smiled. "You have newsprint on your face."

"I do?" I rubbed my cheek. "Is that better?"

Salvador laughed. "Now you have *more* newsprint on your face."

He reached over and touched my cheek and then my nose gently. "There you go," he said softly.

I had never been that close to Salvador before. I realized that his eyes were really black. Most people with eyes that look black turn out to have only very dark brown ones when you get up close.

"Thanks," I said in almost a whisper.

And then over his shoulder I saw that Anna was staring at us.

Friday Night

7:46 P.M.   Jessica and Mr. Wakefield have the first of many battles for control of the TV remote. Mr. Wakefield wins and they flip to a baseball game.

9:10 P.M.   As the *Spectator* meeting is breaking up, Elizabeth sees Steven outside Vito's Pizza. He offers to give her a ride home.

9:11 P.M.   Jessica and Mr. Wakefield agree to switch between the ball game and MTV during commercials. This agreement lasts approximately five minutes.

9:16 P.M.   Salvador comes home and finds that the Doña has invited her fencing class over and twenty people in sweat suits are yelling, *"En garde!"* and staging pretend sword fights in the living room.

"Would you care to join us, Salvador?" a woman asks, extending her sword arm toward him and striking a pose.

Salvador actually considers it just for the sheer humor value, but in the end he makes himself a snack instead.

9:21 P.M.   Jessica and Mr. Wakefield are no longer on speaking terms due to a feud over who got to watch a sitcom and who got to watch another ball game.

9:22 P.M.   Steven and Elizabeth arrive home. Elizabeth drops to her knees and kisses

the pavement of the driveway, never more
thankful to be alive.

9:25 P.M.   Anna comes home and finds that
her parents have already gone to bed. She
walks through the house, flipping out lights,
and sees that the stereo is still on. In the
cassette deck she finds one of the demo
tapes that Tim's band made, the one that
has only Tim's voice on it before the other
instruments were mixed in.

She plays a second of it, long enough
to hear her brother sounding oddly young
and hopeful, as though he doesn't know
what the future holds. Which, of course,
he didn't.

Salvador

On Saturday morning the Doña woke me up by calling from the bottom of the stairs, "Salvador? Salvador?"

"Yeah?" I called back, rolling over to look at the clock. It was almost ten.

"Do you want some pancakes?" the Doña called.

"Sure!" I shouted. "Be right down!"

I rolled out of bed and reached for the jeans I'd worn last night. As I pulled them on I felt something crackle in the front pocket.

I pulled out a folded piece of paper. Charlie had typed a list of the *Spectator* staff's addresses and phone numbers and handed out copies to everyone. I unfolded the sheet of paper and stared at Elizabeth's name and number, even though I'd memorized it last night.

Of course, there were other ways I could have gotten Elizabeth's number, but here it was, just handed to me. Boy, was I glad that Anna convinced me to try out for the *Spectator.*

When I got downstairs, the Doña was just putting a steaming plate of food at my place.

"These look great," I said, sitting down.

"They're maple-pecan pancakes with Vermont syrup," she told me.

I tried not to sigh. Sometimes I wish she wouldn't make everything so fancy. Who wants pecans in their pancakes? But I was wrong, and I knew it after the first bite.

The Doña sat down across from me. "How was the meeting last night?"

"Great," I said. I thought about telling her that anytime I see Elizabeth is great, but that's not the kind of thing you tell your grandmother.

"What's your first assignment?" the Doña asked.

"I'm not quite there yet," I said, chewing. "Unless you consider stuffing envelopes to be the cutting edge of journalism. I think Charlie believes in working your way up. At least for people other than her."

"Charlie?" the Doña said.

"The editor," I said. "Her real name is Charmaine." I swallowed. "How was fencing class?"

She beamed. "Excellent! I'm really mastering the on-guard position. Here, I'll show you."

She jumped up and grabbed her foil off the dining-room sideboard. A foil is a special sword they use in fencing. It's about a yard long, with a blunted tip.

"En garde!" the Doña shouted, crouching next

101

to my chair with one arm crooked upward behind her and the other one pointing the foil at me.

"Very nice," I told her, but she didn't hear me because she was too busy shouting, *"En garde!"* and pointing the foil at imaginary opponents.

"What do you think?" she asked when she stopped for breath. "Am I ready for competition?"

"Well, sure, I guess," I said. "I thought you were going to concentrate on dance competitions this year, though."

"That's true," the Doña said, using the foil to pick lint off the chandelier. "Speaking of music, have you ever heard of a band called Splendora?"

I took another bite of pancake. "Sure."

"Well, they're playing at the Manchester Club," the Doña said, "and my fencing teacher gave me two tickets. Do you want them?" she asked. "I thought you could take Anna."

I cleared my throat. "Uh, sure," I said carefully. "That would be great. I'd love the tickets."

"No sweat," the Doña said.

Just then Juniper, our housekeeper, came in, and the Doña sprang at her, foil extended. *"En garde! En garde,* Juniper! Oh, I'm sorry, I didn't mean to scare you! For heaven's sakes, don't look so pale. Salvador, fetch her a glass of water. Juniper? Juniper?"

Elizabeth

"Hello? Elizabeth?" It was Salvador.

"Hi, Salvador."

"Hi. Hey, guess what? My grandmother gave me these tickets to Splendora—"

"I love Splendora!" I interrupted.

"You do?" he said, sounding happy. "Well, would you like to go? They're playing tonight at the Manchester Club."

"Oh, I'd love to," I said. "Just let me check with my mom."

I plunked the phone down on the table and went to the top of the stairs. My mother was just coming up, carrying a basket of laundry. "Mom, can I go to the Manchester Club with Salvador tonight?"

My mother frowned. "Is that a bar?"

"No, it's a teen club," I said.

"Mom," Steven said from his room. "Elizabeth is only thirteen. She couldn't get into a bar."

My mother ignored him. "Why are you going there?" she asked.

Elizabeth

"Because a band called Splendora's playing," I explained patiently. Why are parents such worriers? I know that it's their job to be responsible and concerned, but really, what did she think we were going to do? Run wild through the streets of Sweet Valley? "It's all teenagers, they don't serve alcohol, and they always have tight security. I've heard it's very safe," I added.

"Oh," my mom said. "Well, all right, I guess. Dad and I can drop you off on our way to the movies."

"Thanks, Mom," I said.

I picked up the phone. "Salvador? I can go. My parents will drop me off."

"Cool," Salvador said. "I'll meet you in front of the Manchester Club at eight, okay?"

"Okay," I said. "Thanks for inviting me."

After we'd hung up I realized I hadn't asked him whether Anna was coming too.

I quickly dialed her number, but all I got was their machine. I hung up without leaving a message. *Anna must be coming,* I reasoned. I was really more her friend than Salvador's—it would be weird for him to invite only me.

Reassured, I went in search of Jessica. She was still in bed but awake, flipping through a hair magazine. "Hey, Jessica," I said. "Want to help me pick out something to wear tonight?"

She looked up at me. "Where are you going?"

"To see Splendora at the Manchester Club," I said excitedly. Normally Jessica doesn't like it when I get invited somewhere she doesn't, but she was going to Lila's tonight, so she wouldn't care what I was doing.

"Really?" Jessica said. "Who are you going with?"

"Salvador."

Jessica whistled. "You two are going on a *date?*"

"No, of course not," I said, annoyed. "I think Anna's probably going too."

"You *think?*"

"I'm pretty sure," I said. "I'm positive, in fact."

"Whatever you say," Jessica said.

We went through the bathroom into my room. "I'll definitely wear my black jeans," I told her. "I just don't know which shirt."

Jessica started flipping through the hangers in my closet. "What about your green T-shirt with the flower on the front?"

I shook my head. "I wore that on the first day of school."

"Hmmm." Jessica flipped through more clothes. "This yellow shirt? No, forget I said that. What about . . . hold on a second."

She disappeared into her room and came back holding up her dark green velvet jacket with the mandarin collar. "What about this?"

Elizabeth

"Are you serious?" I asked. "You'd lend that to me?"

Jessica nodded.

She must really *be in a good mood,* I thought.

"Thanks," I said, taking the jacket.

I held it up and studied myself in the mirror. The jacket darkened my eyes to emerald. It would look great with my black jeans.

"Thanks a lot," I said, meaning it.

But it turned out that Jessica *barely* trusted me. "You can only wear it if you accept the following conditions," she said, ticking them off on her fingers. "First of all, you have to carry a plastic bag. If it starts raining, or if you order something like spaghetti, or if people near you at the concert are smoking, or if it gets rowdy and people start throwing things, you have to take my jacket off and put it in the bag."

This from a girl who washed my best wool cardigan in hot water and turned it into an infant sweater!

The phone rang, and Jessica and I both rushed out into the hall and leaned over the banister as my dad answered the downstairs extension. "Hello?" he said, listened a minute, and then hung up.

"Who was it?" three voices asked him at once: me, Jessica, and my mother.

Elizabeth

"It was a crank call," he said to my mom.

"Really?" she asked. "A heavy breather?"

"No," my dad said. "A male voice said, 'Great brrreaststroke!' and hung up. What do you think that means? Is it some sort of new slang?"

Before I could say anything, Jessica began laughing, really laughing, in a way she hadn't since we started junior high.

From Anna Wang's
Spectator Application:

32. What do you think is the most unfair stereotype?

That Asian people are all very logical and technologically oriented. Anyone who believes that should have been there the day my dad tried to set up our computer. It was like a caveman suddenly finding an electric can opener.

33. What is your greatest weakness?

Vito's pepperoni pizza.

34. Define "peer pressure."

Peer pressure is when people force other people to do things they shouldn't by threatening to stop being friends with them. Peer pressure can do horrible things. For example, it can force an eighteen-year-old boy to lie to his parents and say he's at the library when he's really not, when he's really off meeting some people he thinks are cool and losing his life in the process.

35. Define "justice."

Justice would mean a world where there is no peer pressure.

Jessica

Steven dropped me at the Regency because he was on his way out to look at some used cars. I didn't see Lila in front of the theater when we got there, but I was a few minutes early. I leaned against a pillar and waited for her to show up as Steven peeled out of the parking lot.

"Hi, Jessica," said a shy voice. I looked over. It was Naomi Simms, a girl I knew from SVMS.

"Hi," I said. I'm not sure I'd ever spoken to Naomi before.

I saw three other people from SVMS and said hello to all of them, even if they only looked vaguely familiar. *This is something I missed at junior high,* I realized, *having people know me.*

The theater was starting to fill up, and I hoped Lila and the other Unicorns would show up in time for us to get tickets. I checked my watch. Lila had said to meet here at seven, and it was already ten past.

Jessica

I went inside the theater and checked by the box office and the concession counter, but there was no sign of Lila. I went back outside and leaned against the pillar again.

I saw a couple of people from junior high (was everyone going to the movies tonight?), but I suddenly felt too self-conscious to say hello. Did I look weird standing by myself?

I waited for about five more minutes and then I went back inside to the pay phone. First I called Lila's, but her housekeeper didn't know where she was. Then I called my own house, but there was no answer. By now it was seven-thirty.

I pushed open the glass doors again and went back to my pillar and started scanning faces.

"Jessica?"

I jumped. "Dad!"

My parents were walking up the steps.

"What are you doing out here, honey?" my mom asked. "You were supposed to meet Lila at seven, weren't you?"

"Yes, but she hasn't shown up," I said.

"Have you called her?" my dad asked.

I nodded. "No answer."

"Well, I'm sure they'll be here any second," my mom said. "They're probably just hung up somewhere."

"But what if they aren't?" I asked nervously.

"We'll wait with you until our movie starts and if she's not here, we'll call Steven to come get you," my dad said. "He should be home and he has the car tonight, after all."

"Okay," I said, feeling better now that I had a backup plan. My parents could be really cool sometimes.

"Lila's only thirty minutes late," my mom said, smiling. "That hardly counts as late for her."

"I know."

"Hey, Ned, is that you?" a man said.

My dad turned. "Hey, Al! Nice to see you!"

I didn't even look up. My dad is always running into boring lawyers he knows and getting into boring lawyer conversations with them.

"Al, do you know my wife, Alice?" my dad said. "And our daughter Jessica."

I knew that was my cue to look up and smile politely, but when I raised my head, the smile died on my face.

The man my dad was talking to was standing next to Ronald Rheece.

"Hi, Jessica!" Ronald sang out.

My dad did a little double take. "Do you kids know each other?"

I opened my mouth, but before I could speak, Ronald said, "Jessica's my locker partner!" the same way someone would say, "Jessica's my best friend!" which he (thankfully) didn't say.

"Oh, goodness, this is Jessica?" Mrs. Rheece said, bustling forward to shake my hand. "Ronald talks about you all the time."

How frightening, I thought. "It's nice to meet you," I said formally.

"I just can't get over this coincidence," my mother said, and all the parents got into this tedious discussion about how long my father had known Ronald's father, etc., etc.

I was surprised at how normal Ronald's parents looked. I mean, they seemed about as nerdy as anyone else's parents, but they weren't carrying calculators around with them and they weren't talking about calculus. Maybe Ronald was a throwback to one of his grandparents or something.

I noticed Ronald was staring at me and sort of glowing with happiness. "What movie are you going to see?" he asked.

But I couldn't even answer because I was struck with a sudden horrifying thought: *What if someone sees us?*

Could you imagine? What if someone cool, like Lacey, happened to see me and Ronald and our *parents?* What if people thought that I had come to the movies with my mom and dad like Ronald had? What if they thought we all came

112

together? That would be more shame than I could bear. I would start crying and run into the bathroom.

"Mom, your movie's going to start," I said in a really urgent voice.

"Don't you want us to wait with you?" my mom asked.

"No, I'll be fine," I said. I was practically jumping up and down. "I'll call Steven in two minutes."

"I don't want to leave you standing here," my mom said. "What if he's not there?"

"Then I'll still be here when you get out and you can take me home," I said impatiently. "It's okay. There's no point in you missing your movie."

My dad was still talking to Mr. Rheece. "Let's all sit together," my dad said.

"Good idea," Mr. Rheece agreed.

"If Lila doesn't show, come on in and join us," my dad told me.

"Yeah, Jessica." Ronald smiled at me.

Not in a million years, I thought. "Okay," I said.

Finally my parents gave me quick kisses and they all walked off together. I drew a big breath of relief. Now, if Lila would only get here.

"Jessica?" My heart leaped, but when I turned, it wasn't Lila—it was Lacey Frells.

I closed my eyes and said a quick prayer of

thanks to the God of Good Timing, who had prevented Lacey from seeing me sixty seconds ago. I opened my eyes. "Hi."

Lacey was wearing a pink minidress and sandals. She had on lipstick the same color pink as her dress, and her hair was fuller and curlier than it looked at school. She looked older than thirteen. And she was holding hands with a guy who looked a *lot* older than thirteen, although maybe that was because of all the gel in his hair.

"What are you doing out here?" Lacey asked. I realized everyone else had gone into the theater.

"Oh, I'm waiting for Lila," I said.

Lacey's lips twisted. "The famous Lila."

"Yes," I said, wondering why on earth Lacey had chosen this particular moment to talk to me. Why now, when I was feeling like such a loser? "Lila's in the bathroom. I just came out here to get some fresh air."

"Oh," Lacey said, looking unconvinced. "Well, come on, John," she said to the guy.

The guy gave me a little smile, and they went inside.

I was now completely alone in front of the Regency. I stared out at the sea of parked cars. Lila was nowhere in sight.

Salvador

Elizabeth was waiting for me in front of the Manchester Club, which I had walked to since it was so close to my house. A long line for Splendora had already formed outside, and loud music from the opening band was spilling out the doors.

I waved to Elizabeth from across the street, and she waved back. She was wearing some sort of cool, soft-looking green coat, and her hair was all shiny and bouncy. She looked great.

"You look great," I said when she was within earshot.

"What?" she asked. The music was really loud.

"You look great," I said right in her ear, taking her by the arm and leading her to the end of the line. Her hair tickled my nose.

Elizabeth smiled. "Thanks." She glanced around. "Where's Anna?"

"Anna? She's not coming," I said, feeling a little

sick. "I only had two tickets." *And I really wanted to come with you,* I told her silently.

"Oh," Elizabeth said, looking troubled. "I hope her feelings won't be hurt."

"She understands," I said, hoping this would be true. I should have called her, but I had been so excited about seeing Elizabeth, I forgot. I decided that I would make it up to Anna tomorrow. I would take her to Vito's, just the two of us, and explain everything. I was sure that she would understand having a crush on someone— girls are into that kind of stuff. Besides, I'd never done anything like this before. "Besides, she doesn't like Splendora." I only said that so Elizabeth would stop looking so worried.

"Really? Then I guess it's for the best." Elizabeth perked up. "How was your Saturday?"

I told her about Juniper and the Doña attacking her with her foil.

She burst out laughing, and I thought how pretty she looked when she smiled. I mean, Elizabeth looks beautiful all the time, but she looks extra beautiful when she smiles. All I wanted to do was stand next to her for the rest of my life.

"Hey, who are you going to be partners with when we have biology lab next semester?" I asked, hoping no one else had asked her yet.

"Brian Rainey," Elizabeth said. "He said he

would be my partner if I let him stick his used chewing gum to the inside of our locker door so that he could take a culture from it."

"Oh," I said, wishing I'd thought of doing something smooth like that.

"I guess we'll have swimming next marking period too," Elizabeth said. "My sister has it right now and hates it. Is Miss Scarlett the only gym teacher?"

"Yeah," I said.

"She doesn't seem to like you very much," Elizabeth said, glancing sideways at me. "She always makes you pick up the volleyballs and put away the net."

I grinned. "She *hates* me."

"Why?" Elizabeth asked.

"Because last year I called her Mrs. Peacock."

Elizabeth laughed. "Like in the game Clue?"

"Exactly," I said. "She told the principal it diminished her identity or something, and I got suspended for a day and a half."

Elizabeth laughed again, and a guy in front of us turned to look at her. I didn't blame him. Elizabeth was practically glowing—her hair, her skin, her jacket were all radiant in the soft evening light.

I smiled and felt a sudden surge of affection for the Doña. After all, she had given me these tickets, and this was rapidly becoming the best night of my life.

Jessica

I waited another ten minutes. *This is stupid,* I thought. *If Lila was going to show up, she'd have been here long ago.* If I stayed any longer, all the people who saw me on their way in would see me on their way out. I went inside and called Steven. The line was busy.

I tried four more times, and then I called the operator. "Hello, I need to arrange an emergency breakthrough," I said, and gave some sob story. My voice was actually a little shaky, so I guess I sounded authentic enough.

About thirty seconds later Steven's voice came on the line, sounding all trembly. "Hello?"

"It's me."

"Where are you?" Steven asked. "The hospital?"

"No, the Regency," I said. "I need you to come pick me up."

"That's the emergency?" Steven practically shouted. "There's no car crash?"

"No." Who would've guessed my brother had a heart?

"I can't believe you did that," he said. "I was scared to death."

"Well, the phone was busy," I told him, and rolled my eyes. Honestly, Steven can be so dense.

"I was talking to Lila," Steven said.

"You were?" I asked. "What'd she say?"

"She said that she and her friends were at the Cinemax theater," Steven said. "When I told her that I dropped you off at the Regency, she said that you must've crossed your wires someplace but it didn't matter because *Cool Dudes* was sold out and you should just go straight to her house."

"Oh," I said, thinking, *Why did it take Lila an hour to figure out I wasn't there? And didn't she say the Regency?* "Well, come and get me."

"I'm eating a bowl of Cheerios," he protested. "They'll get all soggy."

"Steven!" I shouted. "I have been waiting at this stupid theater for almost an hour. I want to go to Lila's!"

"Okay, okay," he said. "I'll be there in a few minutes."

It had gotten dark out, so I decided to wait inside the theater until Steven came. I bought a candy bar and ate it, looking out the glass doors.

Jessica

"Hey, what are you still doing here?" asked a voice from behind me.

It was Lacey. I noticed that most of her pink lipstick was gone.

"I'm just leaving, actually," I said.

"Where's *Lila?*" Lacey asked.

"She's in the bathroom," I said. Then I remembered that I had told Lacey that Lila was in the bathroom about half an hour ago. It must sound like Lila had the stomach flu.

"Really?" Lacey said. "Because I was just in there and I didn't see anyone."

A horn honked and I jumped. Glancing over my shoulder, I saw that Steven had pulled up to the curb. "Maybe she's in the one upstairs," I said hurriedly.

Steven rolled down the window and waved for me to come out. Suddenly I didn't care if Lacey believed me or not—all I wanted was to get out of the Regency and never come back.

"Bye," I said.

"Oh, bye, Jessica," Lacey said. Something was different about her voice, but I didn't stop to figure out what. I bolted out to the car and jumped into the passenger seat. For once I was glad when Steven took off at a hundred miles an hour.

Attached to Anna Wang's
Spectator Application:

Textures
Brother is a gentle word,
Like a voice that's singing softly
In the room next door to mine—
Like the hand that bandaged up
My knee when I was nine.

Good-bye is a brutal word,
Like the crunch of metal crashing
Or the sound of breaking glass
Or the quiet scream of silence—
The kind that lasts.

A n n a

"I don't understand it," I said, putting down the phone. "I keep getting Salvador's machine."

"He's probably on his way over here, sweetie," my mother said, putting on her coat. "Why don't you go to the video store without him?"

"What if he comes while I'm gone?" I asked.

"Leave him a note," my father said. "He knows where the spare key is."

"Okay," I said, trying to shake off the nervous feeling that was starting to fill me up. A flash of the night we sat waiting up for Tim went through my mind. What if something had happened to Salvador?

I pushed the thought out of my mind. Salvador was fine. He was just late, that's all. He was totally, totally fine.

To prove that I believed it, I put on an old sweater and wandered down to the video store while my parents left to go play bridge.

You would think that the video store would be a really hopping place at eight o'clock on a Saturday night, but it was actually pretty dead. The only other customer was Brian Rainey.

Brian is one of the most popular people at school, but he's also a genuinely nice person, which is not something you can say about everyone in that crowd.

Brian and I waved to each other awkwardly, and I began browsing through the aisles.

I thought it would be fun to pick out a video without Salvador breathing down my neck and saying, "No chick flicks!" every two seconds.

But thinking about Salvador made me nervous. I hoped he would be at my house by the time I got back. I hoped he was okay. That edge of fear crept over me again, and I decided I'd better hurry up and pick something so I could go home and see if he was there already.

Eventually I chose a sci-fi flick that Salvador would love and went to pay for it. Brian was already at the cash register.

"Hi," I said.

"Hi, Anna," Brian said. "How's it going?"

"Oh, fine," I said.

"You're friends with Elizabeth Wakefield, right?" he said. "She's my locker partner."

I smiled. "She's great, isn't she?"

"Yeah." He smiled back. "Really nice."

I felt kind of proud that Brian approved of my new friend.

The clerk handed Brian his video. "Are you hangin' with Salvador tonight?" he asked me, and when I said yes, he told me to tell him hi. "See you around," Brian said as he left.

"Bye," I replied.

After paying for my video, I stopped at the convenience store next door and bought a bottle of Coke for Salvador and a bottle of Gatorade for myself.

As I walked toward home, I started drinking the Gatorade. I took a slightly different route than the one I'd taken to the video store, and as I neared Sunset Avenue, I could hear really loud music coming from the Manchester Club. I wondered idly what band was playing, and then I turned the corner.

That was exactly when I saw him.

Salvador.

And Elizabeth.

They were standing at the end of the line, not three feet away from me. Elizabeth was wearing a green velvet coat, and even though I could only see her profile, I could tell she looked beautiful. Salvador leaned over to whisper something in her ear.

I stood there, frozen.

Salvador wasn't coming over to my house.

Those words echoed in my mind. *He wasn't*

coming over to my house. He wasn't even thinking about coming over. All day, while I had been look-ing forward to seeing him, and making toffee popcorn for him, and buying him a Coke, and picking out a video, and *worrying* about him, he had been . . . with Elizabeth?

Salvador liked Elizabeth? As a girlfriend? Tears swam in front of my eyes.

Salvador liked Elizabeth better than me?

When was he going to tell me? screamed a voice in my brain. *Was he just going to let me sit at home all night, freaking out when I couldn't get in touch with him? Doesn't he know—doesn't he—get it—*

Fury and humiliation swept through me in a white wave. I felt as though I were shimmering on the pavement as I stood there struggling to control my breathing, which was coming out in gasps that were almost like sobs. I would turn around right now and go home and never speak to either one of them again. I would—I would—

Just then Salvador actually touched Elizabeth. He reached up and brushed a strand of hair off her cheek and tucked it behind her ear.

That gesture broke my paralysis and I did the only thing I could think of.

I doused them both with Gatorade.

Elizabeth

The first thing I thought when I felt the wetness hit my cheek was: *Rain! What about Jessica's jacket?*

And then a split second later I realized that it wasn't rain; it was some sticky green stuff that someone had thrown at us and—

"Anna!" Salvador said.

Anna was standing behind us, her eyes blazing. In my entire life, I have never seen someone look so angry and so hurt at the same time.

"Anna?" I managed to say, blinking back drops of liquid.

Anna had an empty Gatorade bottle in her hand. *Gatorade?* I thought. *Anna threw Gatorade all over me?* She hurled the bottle on the ground, but it didn't break, which only seemed to make her more angry.

Then she turned and ran, disappearing around the corner. It was all over in a matter of seconds.

Elizabeth

I stared helplessly at Salvador. He was soaked with Gatorade too.

The couple in front of us in line had turned around. Luckily I was too confused to be embarrassed.

"Would you like a tissue?" the girl said. She dug around in her purse. "Here, take the whole packet."

"Thanks," I said faintly. I took a tissue and blotted Gatorade from the sleeve of Jessica's ruined jacket.

"Come on," Salvador said gently, leading me out of line. "We'd better go. You're soaked."

"You too," I said. We began walking.

I felt terrible. Anna was my friend. What had just happened? Had I done something to her? Said something?

"Why would Anna have done that?" I asked, my voice breaking.

Salvador shook his head. "I don't know."

"But there has to be a reason!" I insisted.

"Nothing that I can think of." Salvador wiped Gatorade off his face. "Well, unless—"

"Unless what?"

"Well," Salvador hedged. "Sometimes she and I watch videos together on Saturdays."

"Sometimes?" I repeated. I stared at him.

Salvador looked uncomfortable. "Usually, I guess."

"Usually?" I snapped. "Like *always?* Like, maybe she was expecting you tonight?"

"I don't—maybe—I wasn't thinking about Anna," Salvador said.

I was too furious to reply. Anna had been expecting Salvador to come over, and instead she had seen us together. Did she think we had planned to exclude her? I had a sudden, horrible image of Anna waiting at home for someone who never came. How long had she waited? What time had she been expecting him?

I glared at Salvador. "How could you have done that?"

Salvador only stared at his shoes, not speaking. "You'd better get home," he said finally.

"I'm going to call for a ride," I said, and marched toward the phone booth, pushing my sticky hair off my face. I dug around in my purse for a quarter and dialed.

"Hello?"

"Steven, it's me," I said. "I need you to come pick me up."

He sighed. "Hey, Liz, you know those red-and-white buses?"

"What—"

"Those are Dial-a-Ride," Steven said. "Not me."

"Steven," I said, near tears. "I just need you to come pick me up! Please?"

128

Elizabeth

Steven must know what a crying girl sounds like when he hears one because he gave in immediately. "Where are you?"

I swallowed. "Sunset Avenue and Second," I said, looking at a street sign.

"Wait on the northwest corner," Steven said. "I'll be right there."

"Thanks." I hung up and turned around. Salvador was standing behind me. He looked so guilty that I might have felt sorry for him if I hadn't been so angry. I glared at him again and walked to the corner to wait for Steven.

I wiped my eyes with one of the tissues that the girl in line had given me. I would call Anna as soon as I got home and explain everything. Why hadn't I made sure she was coming with us tonight? Had I—had I somehow hoped it would just be me and Salvador?

No, I told myself. I hadn't hoped that—but hadn't I been kind of pleased when it was? Hadn't I liked standing in line talking to him?

I squeezed my eyes shut. *I am not a horrible person,* I told myself. *I never meant for this to happen. I wouldn't hurt Anna's feelings for anything.*

Or for anyone.

Jessica

Unbelievably, when Steven dropped me off at Lila's, no one was home but the house-keeper, so I had to wait some more.

Finally Mr. Fowler pulled into the driveway with a car full of girls. I was so excited to see Lila and Ellen and Rachel and Mandy that I forgot about all the time I'd spent waiting around for them.

"Hi, Jessica," Mr. Fowler said as he got out of the car. "Sorry about the mix-up."

"No problem." What else could I say?

"Hey, Jessica," Lila said, swinging open the back door of the car.

"Lila! Hi—," I said, and then stopped. Getting out of the car behind Lila were three girls I didn't know, all toting overnight bags. Ellen, Rachel, and Mandy were nowhere in sight. For a minute I felt just like I had back in the junior-high cafeteria, when I couldn't find my friends and was about to cry and didn't want anyone to know.

"Jessica," Lila said, gesturing to the girls, "this

is Ashley, Mary, and Courtney."

Right away one of the girls spoke up. "We all spell our names with double *e*'s. We just started that this year when we transferred into SVMS. It was Lila's idea."

So I guess, technically, it was Ashlee, Maree, and Courtnee.

I managed to recover. "Well, it's nice to meet you," I said with a fake smile. I looked at Lila sideways. "Are you Lilee now?"

"No," she said, almost smugly. "I'm still Lila."

I bet. How typical of Lila to think of ways for other people to change their names. I wondered if they hung out together all the time. Lila and the Double E's. It sounded like a band. An annoying band.

"Come on," Lila said as Mr. Fowler unlocked the door. "Let's go up to my room."

We went inside and up the stairs. While the Double E's were spreading out their sleeping bags on Lila's bedroom floor, I followed Lila into the bathroom.

"So, where is everyone?" I whispered.

Lila looked puzzled. "What do you mean?"

"You know," I said. "Ellen, Rachel, Mandy . . . aren't they coming?" I was starting to feel kind of angry. What was Lila's deal? Didn't she know who our friends were anymore?

Jessica

"Rachel had her wisdom teeth out yesterday," Lila said. "And I didn't invite Mandy or Ellen. I thought you'd want to meet these guys. They just made the Boosters."

I bit my lip to keep from screaming, *Look, Lila, I've met enough new people this week to last me a lifetime!* Instead I took a few deep breaths.

Look, I reasoned, *Lila is the person I've missed most, and she's here in front of me.* I went back into the bedroom and spread my own sleeping bag on the floor next to Lila's bed.

"Hey, Jessica," Maree said. "Do you ever go by Jessie?"

Actually, I'm pretty sure she said, "Jessee."

"No," I said coldly. Then I remembered that I wanted to ask Lila about using her mailing address. "No," I said more slowly and a bit more pleasantly. "But I *could.*"

As I plumped up my pillow and stuck it behind me, Courtnee said, "Wasn't Pete Stone hilarious on Friday?"

Lila and the Double E's all began laughing hysterically.

"What did Pete do?" I asked, feeling left out.

"Oh, it was so funny," Ashlee said. "He showed up at school wearing this T-shirt with Greek writing on it, and people kept asking him what the T-shirt said and he wouldn't tell them."

They all began laughing, and I waited, patiently, for the rest of the story.

Maree was the first one to catch her breath. "Well, as the day went on, all the teachers were getting more and more worried that Pete's T-shirt was obscene, especially since he kept saying that he didn't know what the T-shirt said and then absolutely *grinning*. So finally someone complained to the principal, who found a teacher who could translate the T-shirt and—" She paused dramatically.

"And?" I said helpfully. "What did it say?"

Maree smiled. "It said, 'My parents went to Athens and all they brought me back was this lousy T-shirt.'"

They laughed and so did I, even though I didn't think the story was funny. In fact, it was downright *not* funny. *I guess you had to be there,* I thought. Which, of course, I hadn't been. I felt a pang.

"Isn't that new health class disgusting?" Ashlee asked, wrinkling her nose. She was the prettiest of the Double E's, with shoulder-length red hair and just the right amount of freckles.

"Tell me about it," Lila said.

"You have health class?" I asked.

Maree nodded. "Yes, they hired this nurse to come in and talk to us during third hour every day."

"Oh yeah," I said. Suddenly I felt like I could relate to this conversation. "We have health class at my new school too," I said. "And on Thursday the teacher showed us slides of all the microbes that can live in a wet bathing suit."

I expected them to laugh or at least sympathize with me, but the Double E's just looked blank. Only Lila smiled a little.

Then they went back to talking about their health class and the new nurse, and the whole evening went on like that, with them talking and me asking polite questions like, "Really? What happened next?" It was like being back at the junior high, where I didn't know anyone and all of my conversations turned out sounding weird.

I yawned. I'd been up all last night, planning how I could use Lila's mailing address. But I never even had a chance to talk to her about it tonight. The Double E's clung to her like plastic wrap, hanging on her every word. That was probably why Lila liked them.

I lay down on my side and listened to everyone else talk.

"Seriously," Maree was saying. "Did you see some of the girls who tried out for Boosters? What were they *thinking?*"

"Oh, you guys were by far the best," Lila said.

I couldn't stand to hear them talk about the Boosters when I should have been the cocaptain this year. Everything they said reminded me of how awful junior high was and made me feel left out. I decided to close my eyes just for a second.

I woke up the next morning with a sore shoulder and the pattern of Lila's bedroom carpet embedded on my cheek.

Lila and the Double E's were still sleeping. I sat up and looked at Lila. One hand was curled at her chin, and she had a slight smile on her face. I could have woken her and told her my plan to use her mailing address, but it didn't seem like the greatest idea anymore.

Mr. Fowler knocked on Lila's door. "Girls, breakfast!"

Lila groaned and pulled the pillow over her head. The Double E's didn't even stir until Mr. Fowler called a second time. Still, we had to shake Maree awake.

"Ugh," she said, squinting at her watch. "I've only been asleep for four hours!"

A knot formed in my stomach when I heard that. Lila and the Double E's had stayed up for hours after I fell asleep! What had they done? What had they talked about? *Me?*

I hoped not.

We trooped downstairs and the Fowlers' housekeeper served us bacon and eggs.

"Well, girls," Mr. Fowler said, surveying the sleepy faces. "How late did the talk-a-thon go last night?"

Everyone groaned in answer, including me.

Jessica

"On second thought, I don't want to know," he said. "Just hearing Lila and Jessica talk on the phone can give me a sore throat." Then he looked at me. "How's the new school going, Jessica?"

I swallowed a mouthful of scrambled eggs. "It's okay."

"Lila sure misses you," Mr. Fowler said.

I smiled, but the knot in my stomach tightened. It wasn't true and I knew it, even if he didn't.

After breakfast we went upstairs to pack up our stuff and take showers. Everyone's parents were scheduled to pick them up at eleven. Normally I would have called my mom and told her not to come until late afternoon so Lila and I could gossip about everyone else after they left. But I didn't feel like doing that today. And by the way Ashlee climbed onto Lila's bed and began flipping through magazines, I had a sinking feeling that Lila wouldn't want me to stay too.

I took a long, hot shower in Lila's bathroom and put on jeans and a sweatshirt. Then I blew my hair dry with Lila's hair dryer. I always bend over and dry my hair with my head upside down because I get more body that way.

When I straightened up and tossed my hair back over my shoulders, I saw Maree looking at me. She smiled. "You have such pretty hair, Jessee."

But for some reason it didn't sound like a real

compliment. It sounded like . . . well, almost like Maree felt sorry for me or something. For me. Jessica Wakefield.

Luckily I didn't have to say anything because just then Lila came to the door. "Your mom's here, Jessica."

I'd never been happier to hear that sentence, let me tell you. Lila walked me to the door, and we stood there awkwardly for a minute. Suddenly I missed her more than ever. It was a weird feeling because she was standing right there.

"Well, thanks for inviting me," I said, which was dumb—we never said that to each other.

Lila smiled. "I'll call you and we'll definitely hang out this week."

"That'd be great," I told her, but I knew it wouldn't happen. "Well, bye."

"I'll call you," Lila said again.

I just nodded and yelled good-bye to Mr. Fowler in his office. Then I pushed open the Fowlers' front door and stepped out onto the porch.

Our minivan was idling at the curb with my mother at the wheel. Elizabeth sat in the passenger seat with the window rolled down. And she was smiling—not a polite smile, or a mildly interested smile, or a superior smile, but just a regular old everyday smile, like she was happy to see me.

At least some things don't change.

Elizabeth

Nice as it was to have Jessica home, there was something I had to tell her.

"I have good news and bad news," I said, blocking her access to the bathroom door.

Jessica narrowed her eyes. "Is this about my green jacket?"

"Well, yes," I had to admit.

"Gimme the bad news first," Jessica said.

"It, um, got Gatorade spilled on it," I said. She looked really horrified, so I rushed on, "But Mom and I blotted it with club soda and it will be as good as new, when it dries."

Jessica raced past me into the bathroom, where her jacket was hanging from the shower-curtain rod. She examined it carefully. "It looks okay," she said at last. "How did you spill so much Gatorade on it anyway? You're not usually such a slob."

"I wasn't a slob," I protested. "Anna threw it at me."

"Anna?" Jessica repeated. "Your new best

friend? Why did she do that?"

I sighed. I knew Jessica wouldn't give up until she heard the whole story. "Because Salvador stood her up to go out with me, and she saw us together and thought we were both blowing her off or something."

"Well, call her up and explain," Jessica suggested.

"I tried," I said, and swallowed hard. "She won't come to the phone."

Jessica shrugged. "You're better off without them," she said. "El Salvador tricked you, and what's-her-name dumped Gatorade all over my jacket. Who needs friends like that?"

"I know," I said, but inside I felt confused. *I need friends like that,* I thought. At least, I needed the friends I thought they were. Was I going to have to go to school and start all over on Monday? How would I find new friends who made me laugh like that?

"I guess you know your hair is green," Jessica said, interrupting my thoughts.

"It isn't!" I cried. "Really?"

"Just a little," Jessica said. "By your face."

I leaned forward and examined my reflection in the mirror. "That stupid Gatorade."

"Well, club soda will probably work on your hair too," Jessica said. She picked up a bottle that was still in the bathroom from last night.

"Oh, thanks." I gathered my hair onto my head and leaned over the sink.

Jessica poured club soda over my hair and began to work it in with her hands.

"How was Lila's slumber party?" I asked.

"Okay," Jessica said. She paused, her fingers gentle on my scalp. "All in all, I'm glad just to be back here with you."

For some reason, this only made me feel hollowed out inside. Why wasn't anything turning out right lately? Why did Lila always have to let Jessica down? Why wouldn't Anna let me apologize? Why did Salvador have to like me? Why couldn't I just explain to him that I wasn't interested, that I only liked him as a friend, and have that settle everything? Why hadn't I done that from the very moment he invited me to go see Splendora? Why hadn't I spelled it all out then and avoided this whole mess?

"Well, aren't you two a picture," my mom said, grinning, from the doorway.

I smiled shakily at her and heard Jessica laugh. Suddenly I was really grateful for my mother and sister—for my whole family, and all the other people who I'd known forever.

A n n a

On Sunday evening my mom said that she and my dad were going out again. I guess I should have been grateful that my mom has had practically an entire week of good days, but I wasn't in the mood to appreciate it.

"Fine," I said without looking up. I was lying on my bed, pretending to do my algebra homework. I'd been in my room all day.

"Have you spoken to Salvador yet?" my mom asked.

"Nope."

"Honey, I'm sure he had a good reason for not showing up," my mom said.

I wondered what was worse, being betrayed by your friends or having to listen to your mom talk about it.

"I know how much you were looking forward to seeing him," my mom said.

"Yup."

Anna

Around this time my mom, who can be a little slow, picked up on the fact that I was in a bad mood.

"Well, we'll see you later," she said. "I left the number where you can reach us by the phone."

"Bye," I said, suddenly wishing she wouldn't go.

"Bye, sweetie."

After my parents left, I went into the kitchen and poured myself a Coke. The answering machine was blinking, but I had already heard the messages on it. Salvador and Elizabeth had both left multiple messages. Their messages made me so angry—especially Elizabeth's. Salvador at least had the good grace to sound sheepish. *Uh, Anna,* his message said, *I hope you're not mad or anything. . . .*

But Elizabeth just sounds all sugary and concerned. *Oh, Anna, please, call me so I can explain.*

Like she's not going to get a minute's rest until she knows I'm okay! Well, she certainly wasn't worried about how I was last night when she decided to go on a *date* with Salvador. And after I'd said nice things about her to Brian Rainey! But at least she hadn't blown me off to hang out with Salvador. I guess it was even possible that she didn't know that he and I had plans. This realization didn't make me want to call her right away, mind you—I just couldn't bear to talk to her yet. But maybe in a little while . . .

Salvador was a different story. I was *furious* at him. Last night he looked so . . . *enchanted* is the only word I can think of. No wonder he was acting weird all week, changing clothes and being absentminded. Because he has a crush on Elizabeth! Did he even give me a single thought? Did he think, *Gosh, I've spent almost every Saturday night for the past three years with Anna; maybe I should call her and let her know that I'm standing her up to go on a date with her friend?*

My hands tightened on the ice-cube tray I was holding, and suddenly I burst into tears and threw the tray across the room.

How could Salvador do this to me? Hadn't we been friends forever?

The doorbell rang, startling me so much, I stopped crying. We weren't expecting anyone.

The doorbell rang again. "All right," I muttered. I blew my nose on a dish towel and padded through the house to the front door.

"Who is it?" I asked.

"Pizza delivery," said a voice.

"I didn't order a pizza—" I peeked through the peephole.

"I know," Salvador said, holding out a flat white cardboard box. "I did."

"Not interested," I told the closed door.

"But I'm here to apologize," Salvador said.

"Save it for some other girl."

Salvador opened the pizza box and held it out underneath the peephole. There was something written on it in pepperoni. It didn't make any sense, so I opened the door to read it better.

It didn't make any *more* sense up close.

"'I'm a low sal,'" I read out loud. "What's that supposed to mean?"

"I was going to write, 'I'm a low salamander,'" Salvador said. "But I ran out of pepperoni."

I said nothing.

Salvador swallowed. "Do you remember how you used to call me 'salamander' when we were little?" he asked.

I just glared at him.

"Well," Salvador went on. "What I really wanted to write was that I'm a low salamander." He cleared his throat. "Because not even a reptile would stand up his best friend in order to impress some girl."

I narrowed my eyes. "That's not an apology, Salvador. That's a justification."

I turned away and Salvador grabbed my arm. "You're right," he said. "You're—you're totally right." His voice was starting to sound thick. Was he about to start crying? What would I do if he did? I didn't think I could stand to see that, not even after what happened. "How can I possibly apologize for being such a jerk?" he went on.

"For blowing you off? For taking you for granted? For not being there for you when you have been there for me, like, every single time I ever needed you?"

He was trying to look tough, but his eyes were welling up. I bit my lip. "Salvador—"

"Just tell me how to apologize for that and I will," Salvador said. "But you have to tell me because I don't know where to start."

I was silent for a long time. "Okay," I whispered finally. What else could I say? He was my best friend, after all.

Salvador must have been holding his breath. He let it out slowly.

"What now?" Salvador asked softly.

I shrugged. I truly didn't know.

"Do you want me to go?" Salvador asked. "Because I could, but . . . *Titanic* is on cable."

I rubbed one of my feet against the carpet.

"We could watch it, just the two of us," Salvador coaxed. "And I can hand you Kleenex one at a time."

There it was—just what I had wanted all along. Some quality time with my best friend. I guess I should have felt happy, but honestly, it felt kind of weird to be forgiving Salvador when I hadn't let Elizabeth apologize. In fact, I guessed I really needed to apologize to *her.* I hoped her green jacket was okay.

Anna

I felt guilty all of a sudden. On the one hand, I was tempted to blow Elizabeth off and hog Salvador all to myself—she and I could make up tomorrow. But on the other, wouldn't this whole mess with Salvador have been avoided if I'd had more people to hang out with in the first place? Didn't I need *more* friends, not less?

And Elizabeth had never given any indication that she was interested in being Salvador's girl-friend. Had she?

"Are you and Elizabeth, like, going out now?" I asked him.

He gave a little snort-laugh. "No way," he replied. "She's not speaking to me either."

I guess it shouldn't have made me feel so good to know that he'd come to apologize to me first, but it did. That decided it. All of a sudden I was feeling generous. "Okay," I said slowly. "Go put the pizza in the oven. There's something I need to do."

I picked up the telephone and dialed a number. "Hi," I said, and cleared my throat. "Could I please speak to Elizabeth?"

Jessica

Well, my "sister time" with Elizabeth was certainly short-lived. As soon as she got a call from old what's-her-name and El Salvador, she went jackrabbiting over there. (Actually, she rode over there with Steven, who was on his way to—guess what?—go look at more used cars.)

Which meant that I was the only one home to go out to dinner at Happy Burger with my parents, like a loser. But I went because I like hamburgers. On the way over, my parents grilled me about Lila's party and how junior high was going. They looked kind of concerned, my mom especially, but I didn't feel like telling them the whole truth. What could I say?

The thing about getting older is you realize that your parents can't solve all your problems anymore. No matter how much they love you.

The waitress seated us in a big booth.

Jessica

"I want a cheeseburger with bacon," I said to my mom. "Will you order for me? I'm going to put some songs on the jukebox."

"Sure," she said absently, still looking at her menu.

My dad handed me a quarter. "Play 'I Want to Hold Your Hand,' by the Beatles, for me," he said.

"Okay," I said, hoping that there would be a delay or something and no one would associate that song with me.

I went up to the jukebox and began flipping through the selections. I chose one song and was trying to decide on another when a perfectly manicured finger pointed at number 117.

"I like that song," Lacey said.

I stifled a groan—I couldn't believe this. Why did I have to keep running into Lacey all over town? What were the odds of her seeing me every time I was doing something socially lame, like having dinner with my parents? I looked past Lacey and saw a table full of girls. That must be where she was sitting.

The song Lacey had pointed to was "Jailhouse Rock," by Elvis. I privately thought that was about as gross as my dad's choice, but I said, "One-seventeen it is," and punched the numbers into the jukebox. Why was Lacey talking to me anyway? I thought that I would be invisible to her after last night.

"Listen, Jessica," Lacey said, leaning over and catching my eye. "I understand about last night."

What does she understand? I wondered. *That I'm so unpopular, even my best friend leaves me stranded at the movie theater? That I lied? What?*

"Don't worry," Lacey said. She smiled knowingly at me. "I won't tell anyone."

What was she talking about? Who cared? I just wanted to get away from her. "I'd better get back to my parents," I said, edging away.

"About your boyfriend," Lacey said under her breath.

I stopped. "My boyfriend?"

"The one who picked you up," Lacey said.

Ai-yi-yi, did she mean Steven? She thought he was my *boyfriend?*

"You told your parents that you were meeting your friend at the movie, right?" Lacey tilted her head. She was still smiling in that friendly way.

I think my mouth must have dropped open. "I—"

"It's cool," Lacey said. "Having a boyfriend who's old enough to drive. Isn't it?"

He's my brother! I wanted to shout. *He brushes his teeth in the shower! All he ever talks about is used cars!* But for some reason, I heard myself say, "Yeah, it's pretty cool."

Elizabeth

By the time I got to Anna's, the pizza crust was burned, the cheese was rubbery, and the pepperoni was pooled in oil. But it still tasted great.

"So," Salvador said as he ate the last piece. "The deal is that from now on the three of us watch videos together on Saturday night?"

We were sitting around the Wangs' dining-room table. "Right," Anna confirmed.

I took a deep breath, remembering what I'd told myself earlier about Salvador. "And no dates," I said. "We're just friends." Difficult as it was, I made eye contact with him.

Salvador nodded. "Okay. It wouldn't have worked out anyway. You're too nice for me."

I looked at his dancing dark eyes and laughed. Then I stopped. "Shoot."

"What?" Salvador asked.

"I promised myself I wasn't going to laugh at any of your jokes tonight," I said.

"It's impossible to stay angry at Salvador," Anna said, clearing our plates. She said it very simply, as though it were true, a real impossibility.

I smiled at her and she smiled back.

"Well, tell that to Miss Scarlett because she sure holds a grudge." Salvador stretched. "You know what would taste really good right now?"

"What?" Anna asked.

"That toffee popcorn you make sometimes," he said. Anna began laughing really hard. I have no idea why.

"Come on." She pulled him to his feet. "Our movie's about to start."

We went into the living room. Anna and Salvador sat on the sofa, and I went to sit in a chair.

"Hey, sit with us," Anna protested.

"Yeah," Salvador said.

"Okay," I said happily. Salvador scooted over next to Anna, and I sat down next to him.

I sat back, totally happy to be with friends—
these friends. *My* friends.

Anna turned off the lamp, and the movie started. I tried to concentrate, but something very strange was happening. I couldn't understand it at all.

I was suddenly extremely aware of my elbow. There was no reason for this . . . other than the

151

Elizabeth

fact that it was touching Salvador's elbow.

I moved so that our elbows weren't touching anymore, and then my elbow felt cold. *Am I insane?* I wondered. I don't think I'd ever concentrated this much on my elbow in my life.

Salvador let out a long sigh.

"Hey," Anna said, poking him. "We're only two seconds into it. You can't be bored already."

I swallowed. I hoped Salvador was sighing because he was bored. And not because he was wondering what it might be like to be in a darkened room on a couch with me . . . alone.

Not that I was wondering that myself, you understand.

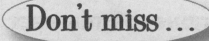

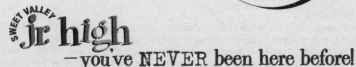

RULES & REGULATIONS FOR THE MEET

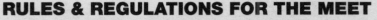

★NSYNC ®

SWEEPSTAKES

I. HOW TO ENTER:
NO PURCHASE NECESSARY. Enter by printing your name, address, phone number, and date of birth on a 3" x 5" index card and mail to: ★*NSYNC* Sweepstakes, BDD BFYR Marketing Department, 1540 Broadway, 20th floor, New York, NY 10036. Entries must be postmarked no later than March 15, 1999. LIMIT ONE ENTRY PER PERSON.

II. ELIGIBILITY:
Sweepstakes is open to residents of the United States and Canada, excluding the province of Quebec, who are 18 years of age or younger as of March 15, 1999. The winner, if Canadian, will be required to answer correctly a time-limited arithmetic skill question in order to receive the prize. All federal, state, and local regulations apply. Void wherever prohibited or restricted by law. Employees of Random House Inc. and BMG; their parent, subsidiaries, and affiliates; and their immediate families and persons living in their household are not eligible to enter this sweepstakes. Random House is not responsible for lost, stolen, illegible, incomplete, postage-due, or misdirected entries.

III. PRIZE:
One winner and a friend, accompanied by a parent/legal guardian, will "win a date" with ★*NSYNC* (date and location to be determined) consisting of a private lunch with the band, a question and answer session, and the opportunity to take photographs (approximate retail value $1,000). Transportation and food provided by BDD BFYR. All other expenses are not included.

IV. WINNER:
Winner will be chosen in a random drawing on or about March 30, 1999, from all eligible entries received within the entry deadline. Odds of winning depend on the number of eligible entries received. Winner will be notified by mail on or about April 15, 1999. No prize substitutions are allowed. Taxes, if any, are the winner's sole responsibility. BDD BFYR RESERVES THE RIGHT TO SUBSTITUTE PRIZES OF EQUAL VALUE IF PRIZES, AS STATED ABOVE, BECOME UNAVAILABLE. In the event that there are an insufficient number of entries, BDD BFYR reserves the right not to award the prize. Winner's parent/legal guardian will be required to execute and return, within 14 days of notification, affidavits of eligibility and release. A noncompliance within that time period or the return of any notification as undeliverable will result in disqualification and the selection of an alternate winner. In the event of any other noncompliance with rules and conditions, prize may be awarded to an alternate winner.

V. RESERVATIONS:
Entering the sweepstakes constitutes consent for the use of the winner's name, likeness, and biographical data for publicity and promotional purposes on behalf of BDD BFYR with no additional compensation or further permission (except where prohibited by law). Other entry names will NOT be used for subsequent mail solicitation. For the name of the winner, available after April 15, 1999, please send a stamped, self-addressed envelope to: BDD BFYR, ★*NSYNC* Sweepstakes Winner, 1540 Broadway, New York, NY 10036.

Win a Date
with
★NSYNC!®

Here's your chance to hang with mega-hot band ★*NSYNC*, up close and in person! One lucky winner will get the chance to have a very special lunch with the band and conduct their own private interview! See rules for details.

Kick back with Justin, J.C., Lance, Chris, and Joey!

Check out the **all-new** ....

Sweet Valley Web site—

www.sweetvalley.com

New Features

Cool Prizes

The **ONLY** official Web site!

Hot Links

And much more!

Bantam
Bantam Doubleday Dell

BFYR 217